R0203003165   04/2022

PALM BEACH COUNTY
LIBRARY SYSTEM
3650 Summit Boulevard
West Palm Beach, FL   33406-4198

W9-CYG-113

Praise for
RED, WHITE, AND WHOLE

"This book is really a marvel—at once so rich and so spare.
A coming-of-age story, a family story, a story of America, of science,
of friendship, of courage, of culture, of aspiration—and all against a
background that I recognize, like seeing my own past refracting in new
ways. It's just so good. Heartbreaking and hopeful, all at once."
—ALI BENJAMIN, National Book Award finalist and
New York Times bestselling author of *The Thing About Jellyfish* and
The Next Great Paulie Fink

"This deeply memorable coming-of-age story weaves Indian
mythology with the relatable modern story of Reha, as she grapples
with identity, family, and what it means to truly be home."
—JOY MCCULLOUGH, author of *Blood Water Paint*; *A Field Guide to
Getting Lost*; and *We Are the Ashes, We Are the Fire*

"A tender-hearted addition to the growing body of literature
about growing up South Asian American. This is a sweet, gentle
story about love and loss, individualism and community, friendship
and family, belonging and longing to live up to one's dreams. In Reha,
LaRocca has created a relatable protagonist who feels caught between
two cultures, but ultimately finds her own way."
—PADMA VENKATRAMAN, award-winning author of
The Bridge Home and *A Time to Dance*

"*Red, White, and Whole* is the lyrical and poignant journey of a first
generation Indian American girl growing up in the eighties. LaRocca
weaves together a beautiful mix of themes—identity, belonging, love,
devastating loss, and eighties pop music rendered in seamless verse. A
book I wish I had growing up in the eighties!"
—VEERA HIRANANDANI, Newbery Honor–winning
author of *The Night Diary*

"Infused with science, eighties music, and the struggles and joys of navigating middle school when you live in two different worlds, *Red, White, and Whole* is delightfully real and achingly beautiful. Reha's story grabbed my heart from the first pages and never let go."
—KATE MESSNER, author of *Breakout* and *Chirp*

"Truly, one of the most heart-expanding stories ever, filled with kindness, music, mythology, all of those things. But above all, here is a story of love, and the ways in which it transcends nationalities, age, science, and fear. In LaRocca's gifted hands, her Reha shows us how to live in the world, even when it feels divided, even then."
—KATHI APPELT, National Book Award finalist and Newbery Honor–winning author of *The Underneath* and *Keeper*

"An ambitious, heartbreaking, soul-satisfying tale of a teen straddling two cultures who, in a time of crisis, learns to navigate a path all her own. Emotionally rich. The seamless blend of ancient Indian folklore and modern western storytelling makes this winner a standout."
—NIKKI GRIMES, author of *Ordinary Hazards* and *Garvey's Choice*

"I had to wait five minutes till I stopped crying to write this, but it was well worth it: *Red, White, and Whole* is a beautiful book that has tapped deep into my heart. It will change how young readers see their world. And that's the best kind of book to read at any age."
—JANE YOLEN, author of *The Devil's Arithmetic, Briar Rose*, and *Mapping the Bones*

"LaRocca's historical novel in verse takes the reader through Reha's past and present, flowing as seamlessly as many of the songs often referred to within the poems. Readers will be changed by her story."
—ALA *BOOKLIST* (starred review)

"LaRocca showcases the best of what verse can do, telling a story that is spare, direct, and true, every word and idea placed with intentional care. A sensitive coming-of-age story with all the makings of a new middle grade classic."
—BOOKPAGE (starred review)

RED, WHITE, and WHOLE

RAJANI LAROCCA

Quill Tree Books
An Imprint of HarperCollinsPublishers

Quill Tree Books is an imprint of HarperCollins Publishers.

Red, White, and Whole
Copyright © 2021 by Rajani LaRocca
All rights reserved. Printed in the United States of America.
No part of this book may be used or reproduced in any manner
whatsoever without written permission except in the case of brief
quotations embodied in critical articles and reviews. For information
address HarperCollins Children's Books, a division of HarperCollins
Publishers, 195 Broadway, New York, NY 10007.
www.harpercollinschildrens.com

Library of Congress Control Number: 2020938967
ISBN 978-0-06-304742-6

Typography by Erin Fitzsimmons
22 23 24 25 26 LSB 10 9 8 7 6

First Edition

*For my parents, Chakravarthy and Kasturi Narasimhan,
who raised me in a new country with love and resilience
and gave me a future as open as the sky.*

Two

I have two lives.
One that is Indian,
one that is not.
I have two best friends.
One who is Indian,
one who is not.

At school I swim in a river of white skin
and blond hair and brown hair
and blue eyes and green eyes and hazel,
school subjects and giggles about boys,
salad and sandwiches.

And on weekends,
I float in a sea of brown skin and black hair and dark eyes,
MTV music videos and giggles about boys,
samosas and sabjis.

In both places I have
gossip and laughter
music and silence
friendship.
But only in one place do I have
my parents.

Give and Take

I am Reha,
born in a pool of my mother's blood,
proper, prim, obediently alive
as she lies close to death.

Because you are here, I must stay,
Amma whispers to me.
To the Lord of Death, she says
Wait a while longer.

To stay for me,
she forfeits all future children,
not just on her behalf,
but Daddy's as well.
Just as she receives something precious,
so much is taken from her.

She says she never regretted it.

Girls Just Want to Have Fun

That's what the song says,
with a catchy melody that makes you sway back and forth.
It's 1983, I'm thirteen.
I just want to be like everyone else
to fit in
to have fun.
I want to free my hair from this ponytail, this braid,
toss it over my shoulders
to unfurl in curly glory.
I want to chew gum,
wear cheap earrings, tight jeans, short skirts,
roller-skate holding hands.
I want to wear a drop-waist dress
to a dance.
I want to have fun.

We are different from Americans, whispers Amma's voice
     in my head.
We work hard,
we dress modestly,
we focus on what is important to succeed.
That is why we came to this country,
and we won't waste our opportunity,
or change who we are.

I listen to my mother.
Always.
But I am American.
I was born here,
it's the only home I know.
So I'm caught between the life I want to lead
and the one she thinks I should.

First Memory

I am three years old,
cradled in Amma's lap with Daddy close by.
We sit on the balcony of our apartment
looking at the night sky.

Daddy takes my hand, points my finger at a silver globe.
Moon, he says.
That's what Amma is named after.
     Moon, I repeat.

Amma takes my hand, points at tiny sparkles
strewn like bright pebbles in the darkness.
Star, she says.
That's what Reha is named after.
     Star, I repeat.
     Which one?
Amma holds my arms apart
All of them, Reha.

    and I embrace the field of light.

Our Home

When my parents first came to America
they lived in New York,
crammed into a tiny apartment
they shared with another couple.
When they talk about those days,
with no money and no space
struggling to find jobs and feel settled,
they smile and laugh,
speaking of feasts made by many hands
shared by the entire floor of the apartment building
cheap movie tickets
staying up late playing cards.

And though we are comfortable now,
with a small house we own
plenty of food
and many friends,
settled and responsible,
I wonder what it was like
to know my parents then
when they were young
and at the start of their adventure.

There aren't as many Indians here
in the small midwestern city where we live.
But there are enough.
Enough to make friends with all,
regardless of language or religion.
According to Daddy,
Indians are famous for disagreeing with each other,
so being friends with everyone
is a gift.

The Star

Reha means *star*.
What kind of star am I?
A distant one, that sparkles coldly from afar?
A red giant, scorching all within its wake?
Or like our sun,
providing light and warmth and life?

But my parents rarely call me by my name.
Instead they call me *kanna*—
dear one,
darling.

Sunny

I don't remember when I first met Sunny.
Her name is Sunita, but no one
ever calls her that.
Amma says
Sunny's family moved to town when I was two years old.
Her mother was already so tired
carrying a baby brother in her belly
and Sunny wouldn't stop running around.
We were only a month apart—
Reha and Sunny,
Sunny and Reha,
almost close enough to be twins.
Amma would bring Sunny to our house and we would play all
    afternoon
while Rupa Auntie napped.

Sunny and I never argue
even though we're so different.
Sunny wears the latest clothes,
has a separate phone line in her room,
dreams of becoming an actress.
I don't think there's much chance of that,
although
she's dramatic enough.

I wish I could go to school with her,
and see her familiar face in the hallways,
the two halves of my life whole for once.
But Amma and Daddy want me at my private school.
You are our only one, they say.
What else would we spend money on?
So my weekdays are at school,
my weekends are with Sunny.

Red and White

I am six years old
perched on Amma's bed
trying not to wrinkle my dark green langa.
We are going to a party at Sunny's house
and Amma is draping a purple sari.
Her hands flip the soft silk
back and forth
back and forth
to make the pleats that will hang
from her waist to her ankles.
The silver border sparkles in the evening light,
light against the darkness of the purple.
Amma looks so lovely,
brighter than the silver,
with her hair loose, flowing down her back
before she captures it in her braid.
Did you wear a white sari at your wedding? I ask.
All the photos are in black and white, so I can't tell.
My wedding sari was red. Want to see?
I nod, and she quickly tucks in the pleats,
tosses the pallu over her shoulder,
kneels at her dresser's bottom drawer,
the one filled with the heaviest saris.

She pulls out a cotton bundle

and unwraps

the most beautiful sari I've ever seen,

a dark, rich red with scattered gold paisleys,

a shiny gold border

wide as my palm.

I gasp with delight.

Red is an auspicious color—lucky—for brides.

Amma smooths her hand over the heavy silk.

I touch, too,

the fabric rich and warm.

I trace around the gold zari work.

What about white? I ask, thinking of wedding dresses on TV,
    in movies.

Christian brides wear white saris,

but we Hindus, we wear white when someone has died,

to mourn.

I wore a white sari when my mother, your pati, died,

long before I was married and you were born.

What about when Thatha died?

I wasn't there, says Amma.

She folds the sari, wraps it in its white cotton cloth, puts it away.

Come, kanna. Let's braid your hair.

I close my eyes.
Her fingers gently pull
on my unruly curls.

Rachel

Rachel is my best friend at school.

Like me, she is different.

She wears glasses and doesn't wear makeup.

And

she is hilarious.

We sit together every day at lunch.

Her jokes make me giggle,

her laugh fills up the corners of the room.

We're in almost all the same classes,

and she is super smart.

Rachel and Reha,

Reha and Rachel,

always together

at school.

Rachel doesn't care what anyone else thinks.

I wish I could be more like her.

What are you doing this weekend? Rachel asks as we walk into
    English class.

Indianing, I say. *Like every weekend.*

Rachel grins. *You know, they say the family that Indians
    together . . .*

. . . stays together, I say, and we both laugh.

This year, in eighth grade,

Ms. Schultz is trying something new.

I've assigned you partners, she says.

Rachel raises her hand. *But Reha and I—*

Always work together. You can try working with someone else.

Rachel rolls her eyes and whispers, *We'll find a way to be partners
    again.*

I take my books and sit at the desk I'm assigned to

and find a boy looking back at me,

his face as still as stone.

Bindi

I am seven years old.
It is Amma's second week at work
in a lab at the hospital.
She puts a small red sticker, a circular bindi,
on her forehead,
then takes it off.
She puts on a smaller bindi, a black one,
then takes that off, too.
She takes an eyebrow pencil
and draws the tiniest black dot.
What are you doing? I ask.
She looks at me in the mirror. *Last week, so many people asked
    about my bindi.*
Why? I ask.
Because they haven't seen one.
Why?
Because there aren't that many people here who are Hindu.
Why?
*Because we come from another country, where your aunties and
    uncles and cousins live.*
*My supervisor asked me to stop wearing my bindi
so my coworkers
and our patients
aren't uncomfortable.*

Does that make you sad?
Yes, kanna.

Amma sighs
takes a tissue
wipes off the dot.

Amma's Orbit

Amma's skin is bright and luminous,
her hair is long, thick, and black like the darkest night.
She wears it in a braid she can sit on.
I didn't get her face, her hair.
I look like Daddy, with frizzy hair that must be tamed
into a ponytail or braids.

Amma is always in motion.
She wakes before Daddy and me,
and makes us a hot breakfast each morning,
cereal or idlis or upma.
Then Amma goes to work, and
most days, she picks me up from school,
gives me warm milk and a snack,
has dinner simmering on the stove well before I'm done with
    homework.
Vegetables, rice, yogurt,
and always tomato rasam,
the sweet sour spicy taste of it,
soaked into rice
or sipped on its own
the black mustard seeds with tiny bursts of flavor.
At night, Amma sews by hand—

fixing hems, reattaching buttons,
embroidering designs on blouses and dresses,
leaving the sewing machine work
for the weekend.
Before she goes to bed,
Amma tucks me in, kisses me.
Good night, kanna. Take rest, study hard, make us proud.

I am trying.

The Discovery

I am eight years old.
I trip and fall down the three brick stairs to our apartment
    building
and scrape all the skin off my right shin.

My parents have just gone inside, haven't heard me fall.
I sit on the pavement, the summer day bright and peaceful
    around me,
wondering why such a big scrape doesn't hurt.
But when I get up to limp to the stairs
I feel the warm blood running down my leg,
and it gives me such a strange feeling,
like I am disconnected from the world.
Amma, I manage to call before I sit on the ground again,
dazed.

Reha! I hear as Amma rushes to me.
That is when it hurts.

All the skin is gone,
and my leg looks like
meat
which we don't even eat,

but I've seen it at the grocery store.

In the emergency room,
the doctor numbs my skin with a spray
before cleaning the wound and bandaging it up.
I like his cheerful smile, his bright brown eyes,
his quick and clever hands,
how he tells me everything he is going to do before he does it.

He explains how the scrape will heal from the inside out,
how the oozing blood helps to clean the wound,
how it brings oxygen and white blood cells to fight germs,
how my skin will grow and cover everything again,
and I will be just fine.

And I know in that moment what I want to be when I grow up.

But
I can't stand the sight of blood.
It brings me right back to that woozy place
between sky and ground,
where flecks float
like dust in a beam of sunlight.

Daddy

Daddy is an engineer who designs buildings that won't fall
    down.
He is logical, precise.
When we're in the car, he gives me math puzzles that I do in my
    head.
When we listen to the radio, he sings along
gets the words all wrong
comes in too early on the choruses,
but that just makes me snicker.

Daddy talks a lot and makes friends easily.
He laughs often, his well-trimmed mustache twitching.
Daddy excels at playing cards, and if I win
it's because I really beat him.

You are smart, Reha, kanna, he says.
But most important, you work hard. That is valued in this country.
You will be anything you want to be.

Drowning

I am ten years old
my lungs are rattling
I have a sharp pain in my chest
that I'm afraid to talk about
because
I'm scared of what it might mean.
My teacher sends me to the school nurse,
the nurse calls Amma,
and she picks me up
and drives me to the doctor.

Pneumonia.

My fever is high, my hands are floating
I am
sinking
drowning.

Amma spoons medicine into me, puts me to bed
and I sleep.
I hear
a soft murmur whispering through grass.
I dream for days, for miles,

across space,

across time,

through infrared and ultraviolet

through constellations

a kaleidoscopic dream

Until

a hand appears,

a dark hand full of promises

I reach for it

and

I wake to soaking clothes

Amma's eyes large,

warm,

shining with love,

Amma's hand cool,

soft,

whisper-gentle,

holding mine.

Welcome back, kanna, she says.

Where had I gone?

Everyone Else

The other girls at school are nice enough,
but sometime last year, they changed.
Teasing their hair into puffy clouds
wearing tiny skirts and heels
painting their nails neon colors
and acting like they don't know the answers in class
even though I know they do.
They giggle all the time,
hang their arms around each other in hallways,
talk loudly at the lockers,
hoping the boys will notice.

I don't have time for such nonsense.
I have things I want to accomplish.

So that leaves Rachel and me,
still raising our hands in class,
still wearing the same clothes as last year,
not worrying about what the boys think.
At least not much.

Our classmates spend their weekends at the mall,

but Rachel and I still spend ours with our parents and
   their friends.
Our friends, too.
Just not the ones from school.

Red, White, and Whole

Amma works in the Hematology lab at the hospital.
She spins the blood and counts the cells
in the Complete Blood Count.
She counts the red cells,

        that carry oxygen,
the platelets,

        that stop bleeding,
and the white cells,

        the warriors protecting us from invaders.
At least
if they're doing what they're supposed to do.
Cells and plasma together are called whole blood,
which is what flows inside us.
Red, white, and whole,
the precious river in our arteries, our veins,
our hearts.

Courtly Love

Pete is my partner in English.
We are reading *The Sword in the Stone*,
and we are required to discuss courtly love from medieval times,
to learn about the society that King Arthur would be ruling.
Ladies were held in the highest honor,
and knights could love noble women from afar,
with no hope of ever marrying them.
The ladies handed small tokens—
an embroidered handkerchief, a ribbon—
to the knights as marks of favor
before tournaments and battles.

I've gone to school with Pete since first grade.
He used to wear glasses,
and once when we were nine,
he fell off the monkey bars,
crashed to the ground.
His glasses broke
and cut his cheek
just underneath his eye.
He stood
with blood
dripping down his face

and calmly walked to the teacher.
He never cried,
never even cried out.
But the world began to buzz around me
and I had to look away.

I was afraid of him
because what kind of creature
could bleed from his face
and not make a sound?

This year, Pete's glasses are gone.
He's switched to contact lenses.
And if I look closely,
I can see a tiny scar high on his cheek.

Pete's eyes change colors
with the day
and his shirt
and his mood.

His eyes are blue,
but on a cloudy day,
they match the sky.
When he wears green,

I see bits of yellow swirling.
When he's arguing a point in class,
his eyes look purple.

Then I stop and remind myself not to stare.
Which is hard,
because Pete is my partner
in English.

Do You Speak Indian?

At the end of French class,
Tiffany comments that I'm so good at languages.
English, French, and
Do you speak Indian?
So many things float through my mind as I watch her twist
a straight, silky lock of blond hair around her finger.

I want to tell her that
people from India,
just the small sample of Indian people in her own city,
speak over a dozen languages.
We are Hindu, Muslim, Christian,
and other religions.
We are all different shades,
from dark brown to almost as pale as she is.
I want to tell her
we make more kinds of delicious food
than she could imagine.
I want to tell her
despite our differences,
we have so much in common
trying to make our lives here.

I want to tell her
I've never studied Tamil and Kannada,
the languages my parents speak.
Never learned to conjugate those verbs,
never learned those curly alphabets.
My parents only talk to me in English.
I want to tell her
when I reach for words
in Kannada or Tamil,
all my brain can come up with
is the French I learn in school,
and what I understand of
the languages my parents speak
is confined
to the mundane conversations of home.
And when I do try to talk,
my accent is wrong,
wronger than my parents' accents
when they speak English.

But I don't tell her
any of this.
Instead, I just say
No.

When You Are Different

you constantly compare.
You hide and wonder
is my hair parted on the right side?
Does this color look good on me?
Should my lips be thinner?
My mother-made clothes are funny
my jeans are not the fashionable kind.
They notice that my hair is black and thick
my eyes are darkest brown
and my skin is different from everyone else's.
Tan, they say.
Wish I weren't so deathly pale.
But I see their stares.
I see their smugness
in their own skins
their own eyes
their own selves
that are so very
Different
from me.

Sisters

Amma loves it here in America
in our little house with just the three of us.
But she misses her older sister, my Prema Auntie,
who still lives in Bangalore.
They speak on the phone every Sunday,
and Daddy never complains about the cost.

There are only two of them now,
Orphaned
but they have each other.
Prema Auntie is married to Vinod Uncle,
but they have no children.
So I am the daughter that my mother shares with her.
The only, only one.
I'm the one who carries
everyone's hope
everyone's expectations.

Brothers

Daddy has three brothers
and on that side, I have six cousins,
and they are all boys.
Three are older,
three are younger,
and I am in the middle.
I see them every few years when we visit India,
and we are going this coming summer
right before I start high school.
Amma saves all her vacation time
so we can go for eight weeks,
and Daddy joins us for the last two.
Each time we go to India my cousins have grown taller,
especially the little ones,
but they stay skinny and quick.
When I sit on the verandah with them playing Carrom
the evening breeze on our necks
as we flick discs across the powdered game table,
when we eat sweet jackfruit dipped in even sweeter honey,
when we play cards late into the night
our laughter echoing through open windows,
I am surrounded by my cousin-brothers,

who call me
sister.
But then I come home,
and I'm alone again.

Only

When you are an only child,
the house is orderly, quiet.
Voices are rarely raised.
Your parents only think of you.
You don't need to share,
to shout,
to seem
anything but what you are.

But
when I visit Sunny's house,
the toys strewn across the living room,
her screech when a brother annoys her,
competition at the dinner table,
I get a glimpse of what I'm missing.
So many together,
and her parents don't notice if she wears lip gloss
or spends too much time on the phone.
I feel exhilaration and exhaustion
when I'm at Sunny's house.

Then I return home,
where

there is no sharing,
no shouting,
only seeming
the way they think I am.
Voices aren't raised,
and the house is so
very
quiet
the way it can
only
be
with an
only
child.

Birthday Parties

are a big deal.
They used to be fun
in elementary school,
with a bunch of girls gathering at someone's house,
a movie, a cake, and presents.

Now they are huge productions,
at restaurants and roller rinks,
and boys are invited, too.
Sometimes the cheese pizza runs out,
and since I can't eat pepperoni or meatball slices,
I end up with only cake and ice cream.

I can't enjoy myself
when I'm worried that the dress that Amma made me,
which is so pretty and fits me perfectly,
is all wrong here
because it's different.
But how can I convince Amma
that I need to wear a T-shirt and jeans
to a party?

Even worse than the parties where I feel so left out

are the ones where
I'm not even invited.

Embarrassing Things

My parents pay for me to go to private school,
but everything else must be a bargain.
We drive thirty extra minutes to buy groceries at the store
    across town
just because the vegetables are cheaper.
Amma tries to haggle everywhere we go,
which may work at the Indian grocery store
(where we buy dal, rice, spices)
but not at Kmart,
where I try to hide behind the cart as she negotiates
with a very confused cashier.

We buy clothes on sale—
never anything cool.
Everything is worn and mended
and worn some more until it falls apart,
or doesn't fit anymore,
the hems inches above my ankles.

And when we see our Indian friends on the weekends,
the parents are always bragging.
Whose child made the honor roll,
who got straight A-pluses.

Can you sing that song for Uncle, sweetie?
I roll my eyes until
I hear Daddy talking about how I want to be a doctor,
and Amma told a doctor at the lab,
and he gave her his old book from medical school,
and Amma brought it home for me.
I barely understand two words in that gigantic book,
but Daddy doesn't tell them that.

Daddy drives
a navy-blue sedan
shaped like a building block,
given to him by his company.
Amma drives
our ancient clunker,
a boatlike creature the color of mud
that groans when we get on the highway.
It takes us where we need to go, says Amma.
I suppose so.
At least the radio works.
I tune it to WPOP
and the music helps me forget
my embarrassment
for just a little bit.

Rules

I don't eat meat.
Rachel doesn't eat pork or bacon,
or any meat with dairy.
We make a joke of it while we study after school:
Bacon?
NO! we both shout.
Cheese?
Oh, YES!
Hamburger?
Yes for me, says Rachel.
No for me, I say.
Cheeseburger?
Pepperoni pizza?
NO, from us both.
We both eat eggs, though.
We whip them up after school into
scrambles
omelettes
fried
poached
and our favorite,
egg curry,
which Amma makes at least once a month.

Hard-boiled eggs floating in a spicy gravy
a miracle of taste,
creamy and flavorful,
sopped up with fragrant rice.

Mustard Seeds

All cooking begins or ends with mustard seeds.
Tiny and black, they contain the perfect pungency
to season a dish.
Sometimes we start with mustard seeds and urad dal,
the black seeds turning gray as they burst in hot oil,
the tiny lentils turning a deep nut brown.
Sometimes we add a pinch of hing,
to give an aromatic taste.
Then we cook the vegetables,
and add coconut at the very end.
Sometimes we finish a dish with mustard seeds,
like with rasam.
We add some of the liquid to the pan in which we popped the
    seeds
so we don't miss a bit of flavor.
Amma is teaching me to cook with mustard seeds,
to take them off the heat at the right time
so they don't burn.
I don't quite have the hang of it yet.
But I am stunned by the world of taste
in something so tiny.

Pop Music

is a game of chance.
What does the DJ feel like playing?
How does he reach into your mind
from the radio station downtown
and pick the perfect song,
exactly what you need to hear?
Sometimes people call in to make requests,
but I don't want to disturb the magic
of hearing the song I want most
without having to ask.

Drumbeats pumping
guitars thrumming
synthesizers bopping
saxophones wailing
and melodies
melodies that make you
melodies that make you throw back your head
and sing for all the world,
with lyrics that are poetry
set to music.

Just like when *The Wizard of Oz* is on TV

and everyone watches,

everyone listens to the same songs.

Pop music connects us—

all my friends,

everyone I know,

Indian and not.

Grandparents, Part 1

My grandfather, my mother's father, died when I was four.
My only memory of him, a train ride
where he held me in his lap, his warm hands on my own.
He talked to me in Tamil, a language I no longer speak,
and filled me with his love.
I can't remember what he said,
just his voice in my ear,
my head against his shoulder,
as the train rattled across the wide countryside of brown and
    green.

My grandmother died when my mother was just a teen,
barely older than me,
long before she was married and I was born.
She was a beautiful lady, a kind mother and loving wife.
Amma shows me photos, and even unsmiling in black and
    white,
I can see the hint of laughter in my pati's eyes.
Amma tells me how she filled the house with music and good
    food,
and left her husband and her daughters bereft
as illness made her sink into the land of pain
where even they could no longer reach her.

Everywhere

Every morning after her shower,
Amma lights lamps and burns incense to honor God
in a little shrine in the prayer room in our basement.
Sometimes I join her on special holidays
like Krishna Jayanti or Ganesha Puja,
when we smell of floral shampoo and dress in bright silk
and I listen to her chant in Sanskrit
as she moves a lamp in a circle
and places a dot of red kumkum on my forehead
with a soft finger.
But on every other day,
every regular day,
Monday through Sunday,
Amma lights the lamps
by herself.
We have no temple in our town,
but Amma says we have temples
in our hearts.

God is everywhere, says Amma.
He is in every living creature.
God has many faces, many forms,
male and female,

human and animal,
and forms we cannot imagine.
This is why we do not hurt people,
or harm animals.
Why we do not eat meat.

God's wisdom is in paper and books.
So we do not disrespect them
or touch them with our feet.

God is everywhere.
And I believe it, because
I hear God in Daddy's humming as he shaves,
feel God in Daddy's kiss good night,
smell God in the silk of Amma's sari,
see God reflected in her shining eyes,
and taste God in the spicy, sweet, piping hot food we eat
    together.

Our parents are God,
their words are law.

Expectations

I am expected to focus on my studies,
which I do,
and I like them.
My family did not come to America
to be mediocre.

I am not expected to like boys.
I am not expected to date.

But all day long on the radio, people sing about falling in love,
about hearts breaking and mending
and breaking again.

And I wonder what it would be like
to follow mine.

Hero

In English, we learn about heroes.
Arthur learns from Merlin, and pulls the sword from the stone.
He is meant to be the hero.
He is meant to lead.
He is meant to be king.

But does being the king's son mean you will be the best leader?
     Pete asks.
Everyone stares at him.
That's a good question, says Ms. Schultz.

I want to ask
Why can't women be heroes?
But I don't.
I just stay quiet and take notes.

Separate

We gather with our Indian friends on the weekends,
dads, moms, and children together
at someone's home.
We nibble snacks and have drinks
until an auntie says to us, *children, come and eat.*
And we'd better come,
or our mothers will find us and feed us by hand.
Once the kids are having dinner,
the men serve themselves, and go to the living room
to eat and drink and talk
while watching TV.
The mothers eat last, usually in the kitchen,
sometimes standing,
always laughing
and cleaning.

No Date Nights for these Indian parents.
They never go out without their children,
not like the parents in my neighborhood
who are so happy to pay me
to watch their little kids
while they go out to dinner,
hold hands at the movies.

Our parents must love each other,
but they never say so.
They never hold hands,
let alone kiss, like people on TV
or the parents of my friends at school.
Our parents tell us they love us,
but to each other, it's like they are roommates
who decided to raise children together.
Their marriages were arranged.
I wonder how different things would be
if they chose their partners.

And I wonder what's in store for me.

Grandparents, Part 2

My father's parents never expected to have a girl of their own
    blood.
They have four sons, and each of them
has only sons.
Except for my father.
When my parents told them they were having a baby,
they suggested only boys' names.
But once I was born, and they learned I was a girl
I think they missed us even more.

After School

On Mondays, Rachel comes to my house after school,
and on Wednesdays I go to Rachel's house
while Amma works her evening shift.
We eat snacks:
crunchy apple slices to scoop up peanut butter,
cheese on Ritz crackers,
or salty, spicy pakoras that Amma fries up quickly.
We finish our homework
and then we do what we always do
before one of our dads picks us up to go home.
We turn on the radio to WPOP, our favorite station,
and we dance.
To the Go-Go's and Cyndi Lauper and the Police,
Bruce Springsteen and Dexys Midnight Runners.
We jump up and down and slide across the floor
    and kick our feet and shake our bodies.
Because it's 1983, and we're thirteen,
and we just want to have fun.

You should come to the middle school dance in November,
    says Rachel.
You've got moves. You'll like it.
She's been to dances before,

at school and at her synagogue,
at Bar and Bat Mitzvahs,
but I've stayed away,
half because I know Amma wouldn't want me to go,
half because I'm terrified
at the thought of dancing in the cafeteria
with everyone else around.

But now
I think of blue eyes turning purple,
and now,
in eighth grade,
I want to go
to the dance.

I just have to ask my parents
for permission.

MTV

We don't have MTV at my house,
but Sunny does.
It's Music Television,
where songs from the radio,
and other songs we've never even heard before,
come to life in music videos on our TVs at home.
The hosts who introduce them are called VJs instead of DJs.
Every weekend Sunny and I spend hours in her basement
sprawled on the floor,
watching magic on the screen.
We turn the volume up to drown out the noise
of her little brothers as they play.

When I tell Sunny about the dance,
her eyes go wide
she jumps off the couch.
You have to go! she says. *I'll help you fix your hair.*
Will you get a new dress?
Is there a boy you want to dance with?

I smile but shake my head.
I don't know
if Amma will let me go.

She has to! cries Sunny.
It will be Totally Radical.

We watch "Der Kommissar" and "Billie Jean" and "Video Killed
    the Radio Star" and "Come On Eileen"
and songs and songs and songs
from all over the world
in an endless loop
while upstairs,
our parents watch grainy old black-and-white Hindi films
on videotape.

It feels like we've already entered the future,
while they only live in the past.

Star Wars

We talk about the Star Wars movies in English class one day.
Ms. Schultz starts off the discussion about the growth of a hero,
and that includes Luke, Han, and Leia,
and at one point everyone weighs in on which movie is their
    favorite.
More than half the class, including me,
names the first movie,
Star Wars: A New Hope.
We've all been obsessed with it since we were seven.
The tale of a farm boy from a nowhere planet rescuing a princess
(and being rescued right back)
defeating the Empire
while making friends—human, alien, and droid,
is the most wonderful kind of story.
As sad as it is when Ben Kenobi dies,
that's when Luke begins to understand the Force, I say.
The parts where Ben's voice comes to Luke give me chills.
Because even though Ben is gone,
he still lives in Luke's heart.
Of the rest of the class,
almost everyone says *Return of the Jedi*
is their favorite.
It's the happy ending everyone wanted,

the redemption of Darth Vader,
the final triumph of Good over Evil,
and, of course,
there are the Ewoks.
It's my second favorite of the movies.
I love happy endings.
There's only one person in class
who chooses
The Empire Strikes Back:
Pete.
It's too sad, says Sarah. *Han is frozen! Luke learns the big bad guy*
is his dad!
It's unfinished, says John. *It's a cliffhanger ending.*
But Pete says, *It's the most interesting movie of the three.*
It's about what happens when the bad guys fight back,
and fight back hard.
It's about learning how to be a hero in spite of the fact
that your dad is the most evil guy in the universe.
He pauses.
The faint white scar under his eye
seems more prominent.
And besides, it made us all want the next movie even more.
Smart marketing.
He chuckles, and the class laughs.
Interesting point, Pete, says Ms. Schultz.

Let's talk more about that second movie, about how the heroes grow,
and how we can apply it to what we've been reading.
The class moves on,
but I can't stop thinking about the look on Pete's face
when he talked about learning Darth Vader
is your father.

Aerogrammes

Amma and Prema Auntie write letters to each other using
  aerogrammes.
They are more than just stationery.
Sky blue and folded into envelopes
like puzzles,
they are secret treasure chests
brimming with words of love.
Amma can spend an hour or more writing an aerogramme letter,
and at the top of each one she writes special words,
small prayers for safety.
She creases the aerogramme carefully,
seals it with her lips like a kiss.

When I find an aerogramme in our mailbox,
I hand it to Amma straightaway,
and watch her face light up as she takes it.
She opens it carefully, so she doesn't tear
  the precious words inside.
She reads it silently to herself first,
then reads it aloud to me,
and it is like Prema Auntie is here talking to us both
about what she is cooking
the new sari she bought

family gossip
weddings and holiday celebrations.

And a small piece of home has flown across the world
and landed in Amma's hands.

Here and There

My friends at school have relatives they get to see all the time.
Even when they need to travel,
it's usually a drive or a short flight away.
They celebrate birthdays with cousins,
have large family gatherings at Thanksgiving and Christmas.

For the three of us to see our family,
we need to fly
from our town to New York,
New York to London,
London to Bombay (with a stop in Kuwait to refuel).
In Bombay we change from the international airport to the
    domestic one
in a bus full of strangers
in the middle of the night.
We drive through the dark city
and I can't understand what anyone is saying,
because they speak Hindi
and I don't.
We finally board our plane to Bangalore in the very early
    morning,
and relief washes over me
as I sit surrounded by people speaking a language

I can finally understand.
Every single one of our relatives comes to the airport to greet us
like celebrities.
My grandparents,
uncles and aunties,
and all my cousins.
And I know I've come home.

But outside my family's smiles and hugs and shy questions,
their chatter and laughter and so so much food,
the rest of the city is full of people who stare
who know I'm different,
not just because of how I dress,
but because of how I talk, and walk,
and breathe.

No matter where I go,
America or India,
I don't quite fit.

Accents

My parents speak perfect English.
They grew up studying it and speaking it with their friends.
Their accents aren't very strong,
but sometimes people act like they are.
They act like they can't understand
when we all know perfectly well that they do.
Baffled Sears salesmen,
bank tellers at the drive-through,
the car mechanic looking at Amma's brakes.
So I am elected translator,
even though all I do
is repeat the exact things
my parents just said.

On the Threshold

I stand between the kitchen and the family room, unsure.
Should I ask them now, or later?
Do not stand there, Reha, says Amma. *Come in or stay out.*
It's the old superstition,
from the myth of the demon who could only be vanquished
neither inside nor outside,
during the day or night,
on earth or in the air.
A metaphor, as Amma says,
for not doing anything halfway.

But I am always halfway,
caught between
the life my parents want
and the one I have to live.
I take a breath, enter the room,
ask my parents
about the dance.

I watch their faces and stay quiet.
I am so good at staying quiet.

Amma frowns.

Let her have fun with her friends, Daddy says.
Reha is a young woman now, Amma says.
She shouldn't be spending time with boys outside of school.

But everyone is going, I think.
Sometimes, I want to be like everyone else.
I am American. I want to do American things.
Sometimes,
I just want to have fun.
But out loud,
I say nothing.

Hot and Cold

When Daddy gets angry,
he flashes hot like a flame that suddenly springs to life,
making you jump and pull back your hand.
He shouts, and we are quiet.
And then,
after a few moments,
it is over,
and he's forgotten what he shouted about.

Amma doesn't get angry often,
but when she does,
her anger is
long-lived
and
slow.
A coldness in her voice,
a kiss that's too brief,
a phrase murmured
when you don't expect it.
She folds into herself,
and turns her face away
like the new moon.
There's nothing to do but wait
until she shows her light again.

And that is exactly what Amma does
after I mention the dance.

Amar Chitra Kathas

When I visit India
and my cousins are at school,
I read to fill the time until they return.
I finish my summer reading list,
and when that is done I read
Agatha Christie and Judy Blume.
But I also love Indian comic books
called Amar Chitra Kathas.
They tell stories
in English
from Indian history—like the story of Ashoka and his wheel,
and mythology—like how Lord Ganesha got his elephant head,
with different artists illustrating each story.
And so, even though I don't know Sanskrit
and I never went to school in India,
I learn about where I'm from.

Savitri, Part 1

My favorite story is about a girl named Savitri,
the daughter of a king and queen who for years
    had prayed for a child.
She was their precious gift,
their dear one,
their darling.
Savitri was so virtuous, that when she came of age,
her father and mother told her
*Choose a husband for yourself, because we are not worthy
    to choose one for you.*
And so Savitri did.
She chose a noble young man named Satyavan,
a prince without a kingdom,
living a peaceful life in the forest with his blind father,
    a deposed king.
But after Savitri had chosen her husband,
a wise man told her to choose again,
because Satyavan was fated to die
in just a year's time.
I have made my choice, said Savitri. *I will not change it now.*
And so she married him.

Cells

I love school,
despite the bad lunches
where I poke at a wilted salad,
crunch on a mealy apple.

I love school,
despite the long days jumping between subjects.
I love English,
The Sword in the Stone,
when King Arthur was just a boy and tutored by Merlin himself.
I love social studies and French and pre-algebra,
where Rachel and I finish our homework in class
and pass notes stealthily under our desks.

But science, oh, science is what I love most.
We study biology, and I lap it up as quickly as my teacher will
    give it to me.
Cells, those magical packets,
the building blocks of everything,
bursting with chemical reactions and molecules that make us
    who we are.
Cells work and grow and multiply,
just the right amount.

They know their places, and work for the good of the whole
   organism.

Science class is like an appetizer,
when what I want is the whole meal.
I want to fast-forward to medical school, when I'll think about
   biology all the time.
But first, I need to figure out how to see blood without fainting.

Amma spends her days spinning blood and counting cells.
She teaches me more than my textbook.
Blood is made of many parts, says Amma:
The liquid serum, which holds antibodies and salts and sugar
and the cells—
red cells, white cells, platelets—
those cells are made in our bone marrow,
the hollow spaces in our bones that aren't actually hollow,
but teeming with life.

You could have been a doctor, I tell her.
Perhaps in another life, she says with a faraway look.
Amma stopped studying science and math in high school.
In college, she studied literature.
She thought she might teach English someday.
But then she married my father without finishing her degree,

moved to America,

and had me.

And here in the US, she found she needed more school,

more certifications,

to teach.

But she could get trained to draw blood

and spin it into its components

much more quickly.

And now although her days are filled with cells and more cells,

her heart is still filled with stories,

the ones she reads each night before bed.

The building blocks she cares most about

are words.

Words can hurt,

and words can heal.

We talk about books and stories and school.

But so much of what I want to tell her

stays unsaid.

My Aerogramme

I pull a blue aerogramme from my desk drawer
    and start to write.

Dear Amma,

    This is the story I want to tell you.

    Once upon a time, there lived a beautiful, intelligent woman in India. She married a handsome, brilliant man, and they left India and moved to America and started their own adventure.

    Eventually they came to live in a small midwestern city. And there, they had a baby girl, and they loved her.

    It wasn't always easy for them to live in a new country, surrounded by different people from where they'd grown up. They missed their families terribly. But they had friends, and they had good jobs, and they sent their daughter to a wonderful school.

    The girl loved her parents, but she also loved the country where she was born and growing up. And sometimes she felt caught between the two worlds she lived in: the one where her parents came from, and the one where they all lived now. Sometimes, she was embarrassed by her parents. Sometimes, she was frustrated that they wouldn't let her do all the things her friends did.

    But she loved her parents, even when she was upset with them.

    And one day, her Amma and Daddy took her aside and said, "You don't have to worry about living in two worlds. You live in

only one world, and that is the world in which we love you. No
matter what your choices are. We raised you, we trust you, and we
love you."

And they all lived happily ever after.

Love,

Your Reha

I seal the envelope,
put it back in my drawer.
I will never send it to her, but writing the words
makes me feel better.

The Project

Pete and I have to work together on a project for English.

A project about heroes,

due in two weeks.

Want to come over after school tomorrow? he asks.

I don't know how to answer.

I live down the street, you know.

I know.

I've seen him walk home and been jealous

that he doesn't need to be driven to and from school,

that he has a kind of freedom I never have, and never will.

       I need to ask my parents, I say.

I go home and ask Amma.

Whose house? When? she asks.

       I tell her. It's a small school, and she knows who Pete is.

Will his mother be home?

       I think so. I hope so!

Then the phone rings, and Amma answers. I can tell it's Pete's

    mom on the other end.

I stop myself from shaking my leg

from pacing the floor.

When Amma hangs up, she says

yes.

Because it is for a school project.

So the next day, I find myself walking down the street with Pete.

His house is old and charming, with ivy creeping up the side,

thick glass panes on the wooden door.

We step inside, and I see

scuffed wooden floors covered in patterned rugs

comfortable couches clothed in soft fabrics

walls dotted with paintings and family photos.

There is a sweet scent in the air.

It all fits together in a way my house doesn't,

with its wall-to-wall carpets and almost-bare walls.

Our photos are on tables,

our furniture is stiff and new, and

there are rooms we never use,

like the living room and dining room.

We go to the kitchen, where Pete's mom pronounces my name
    right,

and I know it's because Pete has coached her.

Ray-haa,

it rolls right off her tongue.

We have grilled cheese sandwiches cut into triangles

and fresh-baked chocolate chip cookies.

By the time we go to the family room to start working on our
    project,

some of my awkwardness has melted away,

despite their fancy house.

Smart

Pete and I work on our project for two weeks.

Sometimes we work in class,

and sometimes I go to Pete's house.

And

he

is

so

smart.

Pete doesn't believe things just because our teacher tells us.

He asks lots of questions,

so many that he sometimes annoys other kids in class.

We talk about what makes a hero,

back in the days of King Arthur, and now,

fictional and real-life.

Together, we decide that a hero:

Is brave, but not without fear.

Because if you fear nothing, how can you be brave?

Says what they believe is right.

Because if you cannot say what you believe in, how

much do you believe in it?

Works to make the world better.

Because doing something is even more important

than talking about it.

Acts out of love for others.

>Because caring for other people is the biggest
>difference between a hero and a villain.

We are talking about Arthur, but I think of Savitri.

She fits all our rules.

Why are you smiling? Pete asks.

So I tell him.

And I can tell by the look on his face

that he thinks

I'm

so

smart

too.

We get an A.

Savitri, Part 2

Savitri married Satyavan.

She went to live with him and his family in exile in the forest.

And there, she spent a year in happiness with her husband.

On the day Satyavan was prophesized to die,

Savitri was with him when he collapsed to the ground.

Savitri laid her husband's head in her lap and waited.

Soon Lord Yama, the God of Death, came to them

and prepared to take away Satyavan's soul

and judge the life he had lived.

For Lord Yama is also Dharmaraja,

the King of Duty.

Lord Yama came with his dark hair

and dark skin

his face shining with Truth,

holding a staff in one hand and a rope in the other.

Please, Lord, said Savitri, *do not take my husband away.*

Lord Yama, recognizing her virtue, took pity on her.

O remarkable and faithful wife, he said,

ask for anything but the life of your husband and it shall be yours.

Restore my father-in-law's eyesight, and his kingdom, said Savitri.

It shall be so, said Lord Yama.

What Rachel Thinks

How was it working with Pete? Rachel asks.

      Great, I say.

I'll bet.

      What does that mean?

You know.

      I know what?

But I know that she knows what I know.

He's cute, she says.

      He's smart, I say.

He's both.

      I nod.

Are your parents letting you go to the dance?

      Dad says yes. But Mom says no.

Rachel sighs.

She's just trying to protect you, I guess.

      I sigh, too.

Deepavali

The festival of light falls in the autumn.
Someone always throws a party, and this year we are the hosts.
Amma has spent all week cooking,
and the other aunties will bring more food,
so we will enjoy
rice and curries,
bread, and
many, many sweets.

We decorate the pathway to our home with twinkling lights.
Inside, Amma lights brass lamps
with cotton wicks soaked in ghee.
She wears a new sari of bright pink and peacock blue,
large gold earrings shaped like bells with tassels.
Her long, thick braid shines in the lamplight.
I am dressed in a long langa of silver gray, also new,
with a border of midnight blue,
and a dark blouse with silver gray accents on the sleeves.
A silver half sari is draped around my waist
    and over my shoulder,
whisper-light and diaphanous as starlight.
Daddy wears a cream kurta that glimmers.

The holiday celebrates
the triumph of light over darkness,
and we invite all our Indian friends
to feast together.
Our house is packed and hot,
full of chatter and laughter,
the low rumble of the uncles,
the aunties gossiping and laughing,
the kids shrieking and chasing each other.

After dinner has been devoured,
the platters of sweets are passed.
Almond barfi, cut into diamond shapes
adorned with silver foil,
jalebis, crisp and dripping with sugar syrup,
round rava laddoos
that crumble in my mouth.

We all go outside into the cool autumn air
to light sparklers.
I stand with Amma and Daddy on one side,
Sunny on the other,
and sparks fly into the night.
We are together in the dark.
Together,
we rival the stars in their brightness.

Always Something There to Remind Me

That's the refrain of the song,
with bells ringing in the background.
I've danced to this song with Rachel,
seen the music video so many times at Sunny's house.
It's about a boy whose girl has broken up with him
and gone away.
But he can't forget her.
It's tender,
wistful,
but somehow,
it makes me happy.
I think the girl will return to that boy.
That song feels like good luck.
Whenever I hear it,
I feel like something wonderful is going to happen.

On Monday when Amma drives me to school,
I hear my lucky song on the radio.
I sing along
and Amma joins me.
Her voice is soft and sweet,
and singing together
makes me feel like I'm telling her some of the things
I can't tell her by talking.

We pull up to school, and before I open the door, I turn to her.

Daddy and I talked about it, Amma says.
He thinks you should go to the dance.
Blood rushes to my face. *What about you? What do you say?*
Amma sighs. *It doesn't matter what I say. You've both made up
    your minds.*
But it matters to me.
Go to school. We can talk about it later, kanna.
I get out of the car and walk to the entrance.

A mother gives you life,
nourishes you,
protects you,
helps you when you're hurt.

But sometimes
it feels like too much.

The Dress

Now that Amma has finally agreed to let me go to the dance,
she's going to make my dress.
We'll go looking for patterns in the store, she says.
We'll buy some beautiful material, with lovely colors.
But days go by, and we haven't gone to the fabric store.
The planning, cooking, and cleaning for Deepavali
    have made Amma tired.
After dinner she barely reads,
goes to bed early.
She sniffles
holds her head
puts on extra sweaters.
She has nosebleeds that won't stop,
and I can't look at her without feeling dizzy
at the blood-soaked tissues she clutches.
Are you all right? I ask.
It's just irritation from a cold. Don't look, or you will faint.
Amma doesn't stay up for *Family Ties,* our favorite TV show.
Even Michael J. Fox playing Alex P. Keaton can't tempt her.
So with two days to go before the dance,
I ask her if I can buy a dress
since she is tired
and time is short.

I have some babysitting money saved, I say and hold my breath.

She looks at me like she can't quite see me.

Yes, kanna. That might be best.

Relief buoys me, and I breathe again.

Amma makes beautiful clothes,

but just once

I don't want to wear a homemade dress.

At the dance, I want to look like everyone else.

At least as far as what I'm wearing.

I jump up and run to the kitchen to call Sunny.

And don't dwell

on how strange it is

that Amma hasn't sewn anything

in weeks.

At the Mall

The mall is a wonderland.
Sunny and I get dropped off by her mom
and stroll through stores filled with crop tops and leggings,
Madonna-like ripped shirts,
lacy tank tops that look like underwear,
all kinds of clothes that would horrify Amma.

Sunny and I bop along to the music,
and I buy
Jordache jeans that fit me perfectly,
and a dress
with a drop waist and a short hemline.
The soft fabric has pale pink stripes
and I feel
bright
and light
like I could float away.

We go to the food court
and when I try to order fries,
the pimple-faced kid behind the counter says,
DO YOU SPEAK ENGLISH?
I look down at my shirt and pants.

What would make him think I didn't?

WHAT WOULD YOU LIKE? he asks at a ridiculous volume.

She speaks English better than you do, Sunny says fiercely.

Come on, Reha, let's eat somewhere else.

I let her lead me away, still stinging, still upset

that I hadn't managed to answer

at all.

Down the Stairs

On the night of the dance, Amma isn't feeling well.
She squints like the light hurts her.
She stands in the foyer with Daddy,
watching me come down the stairs in my new dress.
From high above,
she seems smaller than I remember.
I have on white tights and my patent leather flats.
I've pulled some of my hair back
but let the rest hang loose with curls spilling across my shoulders.
I'm wearing a bit of makeup—
eyeliner and lip gloss,
both borrowed from Sunny.
My earrings jingle as I make my way down,
and I feel strangely shy.
Daddy beams and snaps photos,
but Amma barely glances at me,
then turns away quickly.
She comments on my dress,
says how pretty I am without even really looking.
I know she's angry.
I know she doesn't want me to go to this dance.
But why does she also seem
sad?

She sniffles and wipes her nose
Daddy and I go to the car
as the autumn wind whispers around us.

Come Dancing

The dance carries me away
like a strong current.
The lights are low, and a strobe flashes,
freezing us in poses
like a video on MTV.

A mass of us dance together in the middle of the floor
to Pat Benatar, Eurythmics, Duran Duran.
Pete is jumping up and down right next to me,
and I make myself turn away
so he doesn't think I'm watching him.
Even though I am.
When a slow song comes on, I grab Rachel
pull her to the bathroom
where we giggle desperately.
I don't know what's worse:
if Pete doesn't ask me to dance,
or if he does.
By the time we come out,
"The Safety Dance" is on,
and I can rejoin the crowd.
I do this every time the music slows.

Time After Time

Near the end of the night, a slow song plays,
and Rachel gets asked to dance
by Michael, a boy she thinks is cute.
She raises her eyebrows at me and follows him to the floor
where they hold each other at arm's length,
moving stiffly.
But she has a big smile on her face.

I think I'm safe, standing at the table with sodas and snacks,
Pete nowhere in sight,
when he suddenly appears.
There you are. Finally. Why do you keep disappearing?
I open my mouth scrambling for an explanation, but he doesn't
    let me finish.
Want to dance? he asks in a hurry.
I close my mouth,
nod,
and we walk to the dance floor.
I'm terrified and thrilled
at the same time.
What if I do this wrong?
And what would Amma think?

The song is "Faithfully,"
and as the singer keeps crooning about circuses
I find myself with
Pete's hands on my waist,
my hands clasped behind his neck,
looking up into his eyes that seem so dark now
swaying
and slowly turning
round
and
round.
The song ends a moment later,
and I see Rachel and Michael pull apart and walk away
    separately,
like they are magnets forced together that suddenly repel.

The next song starts playing—
"Time After Time."
The air stills around Pete and me.
All I see is his smile,
all I feel is his hands on my waist,
and he smells
like a magical creature,
a Boy.
We are close enough to talk,
and it is easy, as easy as talking to Rachel.

We don't pull apart until the song finishes
and the moment that was frozen starts moving again.
The music picks up
and I don't want to be dancing anymore.
Want to get some air? Pete asks.
And we head for the door that leads to the patio.

Hands

Pete and I sit on the edge of a brick wall
and look out over the playground where the younger kids play.
The autumn air is cool on my neck.
We slip into talking about our last math test,
what we might read next in English,
whether we will audition for the musical.
(He might. I won't.)
He reaches for my hand
and our fingers intertwine
and my skin starts to tingle all the way up my arm.
How can holding hands
make me feel so alive?
Like rushing over rapids
without wanting to steer?

The End of the Dance

Rachel comes to the patio to tell me the dance is over and it's
   time to go home.
I let go of Pete's hand and we both stand quickly.
See you Monday, says Pete.
Yeah, I say as the heat rises in my face.
Rachel and I go inside together, and she flashes me a secret smile
   and squeezes my arm.
The lights are on, and what was a dance floor is back
   to being a cafeteria.
Even the salad bar's been returned to its place.

We wait at the door for our parents.
But I'm surprised to find Rupa Auntie picking me up.
Sunny is with her, and she can't stand still.
She doesn't look at the decorations in the school entrance
or talk about my dress.
She chews on the sleeve of her sweatshirt.
Where's Daddy? I ask.
Come, Reha, says Auntie. *We'll talk in the car.*
And that is how I find out
that Amma is sick.
She's in the hospital,
and Daddy is with her.

The hospital? I say. I look at Sunny, at the worry in her eyes, and
    my chest clenches.

I think of Amma squinting,

shrinking against the wall.

I thought she was angry, or sad.

But there was something much worse going on.

Is she all right?

I'm bringing you to our house, Rupa Auntie says.

We will wait for your daddy to call.

All my life, I have listened to adults.

All my life, I have done what they wanted.

But I am changing.

And so,

Quietly

Respectfully

I demand to go to the hospital.

And she listens.

What's Wrong

I walk into the emergency room with Rupa Auntie and Sunny.
I'm overwhelmed by its polished white floors,
bright lights, beeping alarms,
and cries for help,
the waiting room full of coughs and bandages,
the odor of disinfectant
masking the smell of sickness and fear.

Amma and Daddy are tucked away in a corner.
She is small in the hospital bed.
She is pale, like the washed-out colors of her hospital gown.
Daddy leans toward her like he's asking her something.
He is holding her hand,
something I've never seen him do before.
When Amma sees me, she smiles
and her face is as bright as the moon.

What's wrong? I think.
What's wrong?
What's wrong?
What's wrong?

I remember how tired Amma has been.

Her early bedtimes,
no sewing,
no books.
I think of her shivering and sniffling
while I've been preoccupied
with dresses and dances.
I can't speak.
I reach for Amma's hand,
for her cool
whisper-gentle
soft hand
that makes me food and clothes
caresses me
cares for me.
My mind flashes briefly to the boy's hand I was just holding

was that also tonight?

Daddy stands, embraces us both.
And Amma says
How was the dance, kanna?

The Diagnosis

Rupa Auntie says goodbye,
that I can come to her home anytime.
Sunny gives me a hug,
says we can watch MTV over the weekend.
I nod numbly.
Finally, the doctor comes to talk to us.
He looks young and tired,
wearing blue scrubs the color of an aerogramme
and a white coat with a notebook sticking out of the pocket.
A red stethoscope is draped across his neck.
He grabs a stool and perches on it,
and his smile reminds me of Rachel,
so I smile back.

We'll need to keep you at the hospital.
Your white blood cell count is very high, and there are some
    abnormal cells.
We will need to do more tests to confirm, but it looks like—
            I know what is wrong with me, Amma says quietly.
Daddy and I look at her in shock, and the young doctor blinks.

Amma starts talking.
She works in the Hematology lab in this very hospital.

In another life, Amma could have been a doctor.
She has guessed her own diagnosis.
And she didn't tell anyone,
not Daddy,
not even me.
The signs were there.
I could have seen them if I hadn't been so busy
with makeup and hairdos,
with English projects.

All our blood cells are born in our bone marrow.
Red cells, white cells, and platelets.
But sometimes one cell doesn't follow the rules.
Instead of leaving room for the others,
sometimes one cell won't stop dividing
until it takes over all the space in the marrow
and spills into the blood.
It's a type of cancer.
And it's called

Leukemia.

The River

Blood
metallic and earthy,
essential,
cleansing,
the river of life
in our veins.
Blood binds us to each other,
as humans,
as kin,
parent to child.
Thicker than water,
it tells all.
The stories of our ancestors are written there.
But what happens
when your own blood
betrays you?

The Moon

My mother's name is Punam, and that means *moon*.
Her face is as bright as a full moon,
always gentle,
always changing, but
predictable.
Like our moon,
she only shows us one face.
The strong one.

Waiting

The weekend is full of waiting.
The doctors take a sample of Amma's bone marrow from her hip
(*It didn't hurt. They numbed everything*, she says)
and do a spinal tap
which sounds awful.
(*I had to curl up like a fern leaf, but it was fine*, she says.)
But we have to wait for other doctors to look at the cells.
Once they know what kind of leukemia she has,
they can figure out how to treat her.
I didn't know there were different kinds.
As it turns out,
I don't know anything at all.

Amma stays in the hospital,
Daddy stays with her,
and I go to Sunny's house.
But it's strange.
Everyone is quiet,
even the little brothers.
Sunny and I park ourselves in her basement,
doing homework while MTV blares in the background.
We keep it on for so many hours that the same videos repeat
over and over.

But we don't care.

I speed through math,

work on my science lab report,

takes notes on my chapter for social studies,

read ahead in English.

Sunny reads for a bit, then paints her nails the color of
   green apple.

I let her paint mine an iridescent pink.

On Sunday, Daddy picks me up and after we visit Amma

(still no news)

we go home so I can pack some clothes.

I will be staying with Sunny's family for the next few days

so Daddy doesn't need to worry

about getting me to and from school

on top of working and visiting the hospital.

And maybe then, Amma will come home, I think.

What about food? I ask.

The aunties have already started bringing food, says Daddy.

Sure enough, when I check in the fridge it is already full of

curries and rice and soups,

almost as much as when we have parties.

The First Day Back

Rupa Auntie drops me off on Monday morning
and we are late.
My school is far from her house,
and she has to wait until her kids get on their buses
before we can leave.
I hurry in the cold
and find Rachel holding the door for me
as I step into the warmth of the entrance.
Were you out of town? I tried to call you, but no one answered.

Everything comes out in a rush
Amma being sick,
how it might be leukemia,
staying at Sunny's house,
and the tears that I haven't cried all weekend
finally fall.

The bell rings, and I start to turn away,
but Rachel hugs me, takes my arm
and brings me to the school office.
We're going to be late.
But she says it doesn't matter,
that I need to tell someone first,
and that's more important.

And by the time we're done and go to second period English,
everyone knows.

Pete pats my shoulder,
and all the other girls,
the ones who seem too caught up with their clothes and hair and
    nails
reach out to squeeze my arm
pull me into hugs
murmur words of encouragement.

And it turns out I have yet another family,
one I never thought to call my own.

The Treatment

On Monday evening, we meet a new doctor,
a cancer doctor
named Dr. Andrews.
She is young.
Brown-haired, brown-eyed behind black-framed glasses,
crisp blouse and skirt underneath her white coat.
Voice strong,
sure,
kind.
We finally find out what Amma has:
Acute Myeloid Leukemia.
Acute, because it happened very recently.
Myeloid, for the type of white blood cell that's growing
    abnormally.
Leukemia, because the abnormal white cells have spilled into the
    blood.

To treat it, Dr. Andrews will give Amma medicine called
Chemotherapy.
Chemo means chemicals.
Therapy means treatment.
Dr. Andrews explains that Amma will get medications through
    her veins

that will kill the cancer cells
that divide so quickly.
But she also says
that the medications kill other types of cells
that divide quickly.
Like hair cells,
    so Amma will lose her hair;
the cells lining the mouth and stomach,
    so Amma will have pain and vomiting and trouble eating;
and the other cells in Amma's bone marrow,
the normal healthy cells that haven't done anything wrong,
    so Amma will be tired and vulnerable to infection.
The medication will make Amma very sick,
so she will need to stay in the hospital while she gets it.

Amma and Daddy ask lots of questions,
and Dr. Andrews answers them all.
I believe in her.
She is the kind of hero I want to be someday.
I only have one question.
How long will my mother need to stay here?
At least two weeks to begin with, says Dr. Andrews. *We'll need to*
    monitor her closely.
I blink in shock.
I thought Amma might come home in a few days.

Amma and Daddy share a look.

A tear slides down my cheek

a tiny drop

that becomes an ocean.

Savitri, Part 3

Lord Yama, the God of Death,
who is also
Dharmaraja, the King of Duty,
prepared once again to take away Satyavan's soul.
Please, O Lord, said Savitri,
do not take my husband away.
Lord Yama, recognizing her virtue,
took pity on her.
O remarkable and faithful wife, he said,
ask again for anything
but the life of your husband
and it shall be yours.
Give my mother-in-law and father-in-law more sons
so their kingdom will have heirs, said Savitri.
It shall be so, said Lord Yama.

The Phone Call

It's time to tell our relatives in India what has happened.
Amma hasn't written an aerogramme this week,
and missed her Sunday call with Prema Auntie.
We know they will worry.

Daddy furrows his brow as he dials the phone.
The operator's voice is tinny like she's on another planet,
not just another country.
Across the world, the phone rings in an odd, rhythmic way
until finally
Prema Auntie answers.
Punam? she says. *Hello? Hello?*
Daddy starts talking in Kannada,
and tells them where Amma is,
but only vague words about what's wrong.
He tells them Amma will be in the hospital for at least a couple
    of weeks.
Once she's satisfied that Amma is all right for the moment,
    Auntie asks:
Are you eating? How is Reha?
Her voice sounds so much like Amma's that I catch my breath.
I'm okay, I say. *We'll see you this summer.*
First, says Prema Auntie, *I will come to help you and Amma.*

I stare at Daddy.

It's expensive for someone to come here from India.

Too expensive.

I will buy the ticket. How soon can you leave? Daddy asks.

We will apply for a visa tomorrow, says Vinod Uncle.

Lost

Daddy's eyes are dark-circled,
his skin ashy gray.
His shirt is done up wrong,
and I have to help him fix it more than once.
In the morning, his hair sticks up every which way,
he barely eats.
Sometimes I catch him walking through our house,
his feet shuffling on the carpet,
like he's searching for something he cannot find.

Daddy doesn't cry,
but his pursed lips
tired eyes
ceaseless pacing
are worse to see than tears.

Don't worry, I tell him. *Dr. Andrews will take care of Amma.*
She'll be back with us soon.
Yes, kanna, he says.

Amma held so much together in our home,
especially Daddy.
He is lost without her.
How did I ever doubt they loved each other?

Two

I have two lives.
One in the hospital,
one outside.
One where Amma is,
one where she used to be.
One where people walk and talk and work and go to school,
and one where they are fighting for their lives,
where the mood depends on lab results on the computer readout.
Amma's white blood cells are decreasing,
the cancer cells are dying,
but the treatment takes its toll.
When I arrive and see her hair cut short like a boy's
so it won't be such a shock when it falls out,
I can't help but cry.
It is just hair, kanna. It will grow back.
Amma is tired,
so tired that moving from her bed to the chair right next to it
makes her stop and catch her breath.
But worst is the pain in her feet and hands,
the numbness that makes her drop things suddenly.
It's good the cups here are plastic, she says with a smile.

If she can smile,
so can I.

Thanksgiving

On Thanksgiving
we don't have mashed potatoes and pumpkin pie,
no mushy stuffing or sweet cranberry sauce.
But we celebrate
with our Indian friends.
With spicy pulao and tart cranberry chutney,
samosas, stuffed parathas,
aloo chole,
and although I've never tasted it,
Tandoori Turkey.

We gather at a friend's house,
and unlike at any other party,
all the dads work
to prepare the turkey.
It has been marinated overnight in yogurt and spices,
and rubbed with more until it is deep red.
Then it's baked in the oven, with frequent basting,
until finally, hours later, it is brought out like a prize,
brown and red and glistening.

Sunny says it tastes good and asks me slyly if I want to try.
And I say with a smile that I'll pass again

and enjoy my tandoori paneer instead.
I miss Amma's presence
and her delicious carrot halwa,
laden with ghee and plump raisins.
But it's good to be in a house packed with people,
voices raised in laughter,
eating together.
I am thankful.
And today, I also allow myself
to hope.

We bring some tempting morsels to Amma,
but she is too nauseous to touch them.

Guilt

is a sluggish stream
that fills my veins,
weighs me down.
My thoughts are full of
should haves.
I should have
noticed there was something wrong
should have
made Amma see a doctor sooner
should have never
worried about two worlds,
when the world with Amma
is the only one that counts
should have never
been embarrassed by the ones who love me most
should have never
written that aerogramme.

I pull it from my drawer
still sealed,
rip it into tiny pieces
precisely the size and shape
of the fragments
of my heart.

I know of one way to fight
the slow pull of guilt.
I think of Savitri
when she tried to save the one she loved
with courage and cleverness,
how she was able to bargain with
the Lord of Death.

The way to fight guilt
is with
Duty,
Virtue.

I am done living in two worlds.
I will be the daughter
my parents want me to be.

Dutiful

I return to school
more focused than ever before.
I will learn everything there is to learn
not just for knowledge
not just for grades
because I want to be the best
at the things that matter most
to Amma and Daddy
and me.
The important things.
I check my homework three times,
pay attention to the teachers,
raise my hand as much as possible.
I stop passing notes to Rachel in math class.
Ms. Schultz has made us change partners in English,
so I stop talking to Pete completely.
He tries to catch me in the hallways,
approaches me at lunch,
but I pretend I haven't heard
and after a while,
he stops trying.

I barely remember
the warmth of his hand
on a cool autumn night.

Under Hospital Lights

it's always daytime,
even at night.
Nurses step into rooms
to check temperatures, blood pressures.
When it's time for medicine,
they pour pills into Amma's hand from a little paper cup,
and it reminds me of the ones we use in school
for fluoride rinses.
Each morning and evening,
the doctors come along,
Dr. Andrews with two or three students,
to ask Amma how she is feeling
(Better. Good.)
and listen to her breathing and heartbeat
through their stethoscopes.
Amma tells them I want to be a doctor,
and they explain everything to me in ways I can understand,
or at least pretend to.

Under hospital lights,
Amma's skin is dull,
hair brittle,
eyes shadowed.

But her voice is the same,
sweet and melodic
over the ceaseless beeping of machines
in the hall.

Under hospital lights,
a bag of fluid drip drip drips
through a plastic tube into Amma's arm.
One evening when Daddy and I visit,
a nurse comes in behind us,
and what she hangs on the metal pole near the bed
is not a bag of fluid,
but a bag of blood.
I see it and
the world turns gray
with specks of light floating in the corners.
Reha! Amma cries.
The next thing I know,
I am lying on the floor of Amma's hospital room
Daddy holding an ice pack to my neck,
the nurse bending my legs.
Are you all right, kanna? Amma asks.
Even though
she's the one who's sick.

Under hospital lights,
the world is upside down.
The world of medicine,
the one I've always wanted to join,
is scary.
And I begin to question
whether I really want to be a part of it.

Not Allowed

Prema Auntie is not allowed to visit.
She has not been able to get a visa
to come to the US to help us.
The men at the American embassy don't believe her
when she says she has no intention of staying in the US forever,
that she leaves a husband and relatives and friends in India,
that India is her home,
that she needs to come to America to see her only sister
   while she is ill,
needs to help her sister's family,
and then she will return.
She asks us to get a letter from Dr. Andrews
to help convince them.
So Dr. Andrews writes a letter
that explains Amma is gravely ill
and we send it to India via courier.
Gravely ill.
I cannot get the words out of my head.
I want Prema Auntie to visit,
but I wish it weren't for this reason.

The New Routine

On every day but Wednesday,
Daddy has to leave work early to pick me up from school.
Rupa Auntie offered, but she lives so far away
and has her own three kids who arrive home at different times
and need to go to piano and gymnastics and dance.
And while other aunties offered,
we aren't close enough to them
to accept this kind of favor.
I worry about Daddy.
There's a crease in his forehead that never goes away.
We listen to the radio in the car
but he doesn't sing,
not even to his favorite band, Pink Floyd.
And after we get home,
he gets on the phone
to call his office and talk to the people who are doing the work
that he's supposed to be doing.
Later,
we go to the hospital to visit Amma.
She doesn't eat because it hurts,
and we don't eat
because she hurts.
When we come home at night,

sometimes we reheat what the aunties have made.
But mostly we just drink water,
eat a piece of fruit,
and stumble to bed
to do it all over again the next day.
I dream that I am
sinking
and there is no bottom.

Mustard Seeds, Part 2

The week after Thanksgiving, I say
the aunties cannot feed us forever,
even though they want to.
We need to make our own food.

And so, Daddy and I attempt to make rasam.
The pressure cooker spits steam,
the dal is cooked.
We add water and tomatoes,
rasam powder,
salt,
sour tamarind,
and bring it all to a boil.
It almost smells like Amma's rasam,
but not quite.
All that is left is the mustard seeds.
I take the small pan that Amma always uses
    and put it on the stove.
I pour in a bit of oil, scoop a spoon of mustard seeds,
cover the pan with a lid
and listen for the sound of popping.
I stand there,
alert

waiting to switch the burner off.
But when I lift the lid,
a horrible scorched scent assaults my nose.
I bring the pan to the sink.
It hisses as the water hits it
and the awful smell hangs in the air.
It's okay, says Daddy. *We can try again.*
But it's not okay. My appetite is gone.
Everything is ruined.

Two Weeks

All of Amma's hair is gone,
even her eyebrows and eyelashes.
Her face is thin,
her skin see-through.
The hospital staff knows she is vegetarian,
but the kitchen keeps sending up meals of
turkey with stuffing and gravy
baked chicken
meat loaf.
She never complains, but I look at her tray every day when I visit
and I realize all she's eating is mashed potatoes.
We can bring you food, I offer. *Rupa Auntie keeps cooking for us.*
My mouth is too sore, she says.
Two weeks after she started chemotherapy,
she has another bone marrow biopsy.
(*It didn't hurt*, she says.)
But she doesn't get to come home yet.
We wait four more days
to find out
the chemotherapy didn't work,
the cancer cells are still there,
invading,
ugly.

Won't Make Her Come Home

I'm at my locker putting away books before lunch.
The corridor clears out
as I fumble with the lock.
I don't care if I'm late.
I'm not hungry, anyway.

When I finally close my locker door,
Pete is nearby,
looking at me with storm cloud eyes.
How are you? he asks.

                Fine.
I don't believe you.

                It's none of your business.
Aren't we friends? I want to help.

                You can't help. I've got to go. I turn to go.
Not talking to me won't make her come home any faster.

I stalk away and don't turn back.
A tornado brews in my chest and I want to scream.
What does Pete know, anyway?

Please

Amma spikes a fever,
develops a terrible cough,
gets so sick
she can't breathe on her own.
So she's taken to a place on another floor,
called the Intensive Care Unit,
and put on a breathing machine.
She has pneumonia,
much worse than I ever had.

When Dr. Andrews talks to Daddy,
her face sags.
I sink into a chair,
pull my legs up and hug them
like a little kid.

I close my eyes,
think of Savitri,
how she tried to save the one she loved
with courage, cleverness,
virtue.

Please, I think.

If I am virtuous, if I follow all the rules.
Please
Please
Please.

Suddenly, I can't stand the smell of the hospital,
the dry, dead air,
the sound of the breathing machine,
the feel of my own skin.
I rush to a bathroom,
splash cold water on my face.
I barely recognize myself in the mirror.

Please, I whisper every morning
Please, I say as I light the lamps
Please, I whisper into my pillow at night
Please let me be virtuous enough.

The Color of Virtue

If virtue has a color, it's not white.
Not that pale, all-reflecting non-hue,
not that color of mourning.

If virtue has a color,
it's the color of the life within us,
dancing with every heartbeat.
It's the legacy of our ancestors,
the gifts of our parents
that we try to live up to.

If virtue has a color,
it's an auspicious one.
Red.
Blood red.

Wednesday

Every day I wake early
shower and light the lamps
trying to remember the words that Amma used to say,
trying to mimic her motions exactly.
Daddy and I eat cold cereal.
He gulps his coffee and we're off to school,
where he drops me off super early
so he can get to work ahead of everyone else.
I read in the office until
I can go to homeroom,
where Rachel and I see each other before class starts.
We talk about schoolwork—
What did you get for number five?
And TV shows—
But I haven't watched anything in a while.

I look forward to Wednesday afternoon,
when I go to Rachel's house.
But although we eat the same snacks,
finish our homework together,
and listen to music on WPOP—
Bonnie Tyler,
Prince,

Spandau Ballet,
I don't feel like dancing anymore.
I don't think I ever will.

School Daze

Everyone at school is kind to me.
Classmates, teachers,
even the principal and office staff
ask me how Amma is.
Better. Good, I lie.
The truth is,
things are terrible.
Amma is still in the ICU,
still having fevers every day,
still not breathing on her own.
But I don't want to talk
about Amma and her illness.

When I'm at school,
I want to dive into the river of my classes.
I want to balance equations,
conjugate French verbs,
discuss Civil War battles,
consider xylem and phloem inside plants.
I want to lose myself in my English book,
think about heroes and adventure,
not my own sadness,
my own worries,
my own desperate hope.

Everything has changed,
my old life has floated away.
I hold on to school,
to its familiar routines,
like a life raft
but I feel myself being pulled under.

One day when Daddy picks me up
late
tired,
worried,
hurrying from work,
Pete's mom stops him at the school entrance
and Pete comes up to me.
I don't want to talk to him,
but I can't be rude in front of parents.

He says,
Have you read chapter seven yet in English?
I'm not finished, I say, looking at Daddy and Mrs. Brown.
Have you gotten to the part where—
Don't tell me. I want to be surprised.
Okay, he says.
I risk a brief glance. Today his eyes are swirled with green.
Daddy and Pete's mom wave us over.

Reha, says Mrs. Brown, *would you like to come to our house in the*
    afternoons? You can do homework with Pete, and your dad can
    pick you up in the evening after work. You can even stay
    for dinner, anytime you like.

You need a break, Reha, says Daddy. His eyes are full of hope.
He needs a break, too.
He can't keep leaving work early every day.
We can't keep asking friends to drive across town to pick me up.
Thank you, I say, blinking back tears.
                I feel Pete release a breath.

Afternoons

are mine again.
I walk home with Pete after school
to his cozy house.
His mom always has a snack waiting for us—
veggies and onion dip,
fancy crackers topped with salty cheese,
tiny sandwiches with the crusts cut off.
And fresh-baked cookies:
chocolate chip, oatmeal raisin,
or my favorite, that she calls
Kitchen Sink,
which have a little bit of everything thrown in.
We listen to music while we eat snacks
and do our homework.
I meet Pete's older sister, Penelope,
who likes to wear black and has pierced her ears many times.
Don't ever call her Penny, Pete warns. *She'll turn into a monster
    and bite your head off.*
But he doesn't have to worry.
I think Penelope is a beautiful name,
a warrior princess hero,
and I'd never dream of shortening it.
Penelope likes me, too.

Although she always changes the radio station
when she comes into the room.

Pete and I finish our homework. He is just as smart
    as I remember.
And I smile, because why wouldn't he be?
Did I say something funny? he asks.
No, I say, the smile still on my face.
Good. I wasn't trying to be funny.
He covers his mouth with his hand
and breathes like Darth Vader.

And I laugh out loud
startling myself
with the unfamiliar noise.

True

Amma is still desperately sick
with pneumonia.
She is still in the ICU,
not getting better
despite all the treatments the doctors try.
My visits are restricted to only a few minutes,
which, I'm embarrassed to say,
is a relief.
Amma is asleep,
her breathing controlled by a machine.
My chest hurts when I see her like this,
my Amma, who was always in motion,
lying so still,
moving only when a machine pushes air into her lungs.
Though I make sure not to watch while blood is drawn,
the feel of the ICU
makes me sick to my stomach,
dizzy,
weak.
How can I be a doctor
if this is how the hospital affects me?

Daddy can see all this on my face.

He tells me I shouldn't visit every day,
that I need to do things that make me happy.
But how can I be happy
when Amma is so sick?

I'm afraid
that she will never leave the hospital
that nothing will ever be normal again.

Will Amma die?
I'm afraid to ask Daddy,
because I'm scared
that might make it come true.
And if Amma dies, what happens to her then?

I ask Sunny,
who says, *Maybe she'll be reincarnated,*
as a new baby somewhere,
or a bird,
or a butterfly.
Or maybe she'll be one with God.

Pete says,
I've been taught that good people like your mom
go to heaven.

Rachel looks at me seriously.
People say all kinds of things,
but I don't know.

The truth is,
no one knows.

But, says Rachel, *we remember my grandfather each year on the*
*   day of his death.*
We light a candle and think about him and talk about him all day
*   as it burns.*
So in a way, he's still with us.
But maybe, Reha, you don't need to think about this right now.

The Promise

I am seven years old.

Daddy is sick, his belly hurts.

We all go to the emergency room,

and learn that he must have his appendix out.

Now.

I am full of questions.

Why? Who will do the surgery? What if Daddy doesn't want it out?

What will happen?

Will Daddy be all right?

Daddy will be fine, says Amma. *The doctors know exactly how*
*   to take an appendix out.*

What if Daddy dies?

It is the worst thing I can imagine.

He will not. The doctors—

What if Daddy dies?

Amma pauses, picks me up, looks in my eyes.

Then I will be both mother and father to you.

I will take care of you, Reha, kanna.

Always.

We go home and I tuck into bed right next to her.

I don't remember my dreams

but I know they aren't scary.

Daddy has the surgery the next morning,
and he is fine.

Rapids

One day Daddy calls and says he will be late
so I stay for dinner
at Pete's house.
I feel a pang at not seeing Amma,
but she is still asleep in the ICU.
Pete's mom makes a big meal:
salad with croutons she made herself,
spaghetti with a spicy red sauce,
meatballs on the side.
We sprinkle our pasta with parmesan cheese
from a dish
not a green container like at school,
scoop up the last bits of sauce with garlic bread.
We talk,
Pete, Penelope, Mrs. Brown, and me,
and I can't help glancing at the empty chair.
Is Mr. Brown stuck at work, too? I ask.
Everyone stiffens.
He doesn't live here anymore, says Mrs. Brown.
I'm sorry, I say.
She smiles reassuringly.
It's okay, Reha. It's still something we're getting used to.
And just like that,

our easy conversation has disappeared.

Later, Pete and I listen to music
on a boom box
in his basement.
He left for good just a month ago, Pete says.
He lives in an apartment downtown.
I'm sorry, I say again.
Pete's jaw tightens. *He says it's better this way.* His voice cracks.
I say nothing.
I have to spend every other weekend with him.
He's split us apart
and we'll never be the same again.
What can I say?
I haven't cried in years. Do you know why?
I shake my head,
remember Pete bleeding from his face,
walking calmly to the teacher.
He doesn't like crying, Pete says,
his eyes wet.

He reaches for my hand,
and I take it.
My arm doesn't tingle,
because it doesn't feel strange.

And I realize
we are friends,
both
living two lives,
both
rushing over rapids
in separate boats.

The Arrival

On the Sunday before Christmas,
Sunny and I are watching MTV when
"Always Something There to Remind Me" comes on.
If I close my eyes,
I can hear Amma singing the refrain
in the car.
It's still my lucky song,
but there's only one kind of luck
that I want now.

Later,
Daddy comes downstairs to Sunny's basement.
Reha, I have a surprise, he says.

Hello, Reha, comes a voice that sounds like Amma's.
And I'm standing.
I'm rushing to her,
to my aunt,
to Amma's only sister,
falling into her embrace.

She's the same height as Amma.

She smells of sandalwood and coconut and silk.

My Prema Auntie.

I am here, she says. *Everything will be all right.*

Another Surprise

We leave Sunny's house and go straight to the hospital.
When we get there,
we find another surprise.
Amma is still in the ICU,
but she's off the breathing machine
and she is awake.

I rush to Amma, embrace her gently
around the wires and tubes she's connected to,
kiss her and tell her I love her a million times.
I drink up her pale skin, her dark eyes,
the smile curving on her face.

Prema Auntie has come,
and just maybe
everything will
be all right.

My Mother's Sister

Punam, Auntie says,
stroking my mother's cheek.
I have to look away
at the love I see between them.
Daddy and I leave the room and let them talk
about whatever sisters share at these kinds of times.
And when we leave the hospital,
Amma's face is brighter,
a dimmed moon
slowly waxing.

Prema Auntie's voice sounds just like Amma's,
but she doesn't look that much like Amma.
Her nose is sharper, her eyes lighter,
her hair curlier, and not as long.
But she has Amma's endless energy.

As soon as we get home,
Prema Auntie looks in our refrigerator and shakes her head.
Take me to the market to buy food, she says.
You must be tired after your long journey, says Daddy. *Take some
    rest.*
I cannot rest until I make sure you and Reha have eaten properly.

I am here to care for all of you.

So we go to Kroger.

Auntie looks at the vegetables, raises an eyebrow

as she picks up a huge eggplant, dark as a bruise.

Everything is so big here.

Yes, but they don't taste the same, I say.

All the vegetables in India taste better,

like growing them bigger here has sapped them of their flavor.

I brought some new masala with me, says Auntie.

We'll see how good they taste with that.

Before we know it, we are home,

and the kitchen is filled with familiar smells:

rice steaming in the pressure cooker,

rasam simmering on the stove,

and new smells,

like the eggplant Auntie has cooked with the new masala.

We eat together,

the piping hot spicy sweet food,

for the first time in what feels like

forever.

Roommates

Prema Auntie asks if she can sleep in my bed with me.
And I have a double bed, so I say yes.
It relaxes and relieves me to hear her breathing next to me,
to see her sleeping form, so much like my Amma.
In the dark,
she gropes for my hand,
and I hold on.
I haven't slept this well in weeks.

The New Rhythm

With Prema Auntie at home,
we fall into a rhythm.
She wakes early to light the lamps,
and I light them with her.
She gives us a hot breakfast,
idlis or upma,
sometimes even mini dosas.

I go to school and dive into my subjects.
I concentrate with all my mind,
and reading and discussing and writing bring me joy,
a dam to hold back the worry in my heart.
I work hard to make Amma proud,
to be the most virtuous daughter.

Since Prema Auntie cannot drive,
my afternoons are still spent at Pete's or Rachel's.
And when Daddy brings me home,
Prema Auntie is ready with tea and snacks, which she calls *tiffin*.
We pack things up to bring to the hospital for Amma.

Amma has recovered from her pneumonia
and is back in her regular room where we can all visit again.

Did you feel like you were drowning? I ask.
I can't remember, she says.
She starts another round of chemotherapy
to fight the cancer.
She is still weak,
too weak to sew or read or watch TV.
Sometimes I read to her,
from my English books or Amar Chitra Kathas
or even my science text.

Prema Auntie makes soft, bland food,
rice and dal and mushy vegetables,
and feeds them to Amma like she is a little bird.
And Amma eats.
Her face fills out a little more,
her sleep seems deeper,
her energy better.
All the nurses ask if they can have the recipes
so they can try them.
The next day, Prema Auntie
brings enough food for the nurses as well.
My auntie doesn't have a child of her own,
so she takes care of everyone around her
like we are all her children.

Pop or Alternative

Pete's house is a refuge.
Somehow,
nothing is awkward anymore.
We spend hours working on homework
while we listen to our favorite pop music station,
unless Penelope is in the room,
and she insists on listening to the alternative music station
   instead.
Pete rolls his eyes, but I like the songs by
Echo and the Bunnymen,
R.E.M.,
the Cure.
Alternative is just pop
that's liked by a different group of people.
As soon as Penelope leaves, Pete turns it back to WPOP,
to the Go-Go's,
Def Leppard,
Cyndi Lauper.
We never mention the dance.

Every Breath You Take

We aren't Christian,
but we celebrate Christmas
because everyone does.
This year it is strange without Amma,
but on Christmas Eve,
Daddy brings up the tree from the basement,
and we decorate it with lights and sparkly garlands
   and ornaments—
simple glass globes,
and all the messy ones I've made in school through the years.
We listen to Hindi film songs instead of Christmas carols,
and Daddy sings along
and comes in too early on all the choruses.
Prema Auntie cooks us a feast:
malai kofta in a creamy sauce,
green pulao rice,
chana masala,
fresh chapatis she pulls hot from the pan.
It feels festive in an odd way.
There is an empty space where Amma should be.

On Christmas morning,
we open presents in our pajamas,

Daddy, Prema Auntie, and me,

sitting on the floor underneath the tree.

I give Daddy fancy shaving cream I picked up in the mall,

and leather driving gloves lined with soft wool.

For Prema Auntie, I've selected the nicest-smelling perfume
  I could find,

and three pairs of thick socks for her to wear
    through our cold winter.

Prema Auntie gives me a scarf

with different shades of blue swirled together like sherbet,

so soft against my skin.

I know she has knitted it herself,

in the hours I've been away at school.

From Amma and me, Daddy says,

bringing me a stack of presents.

I exclaim over two new sweaters

a pretty blouse

and a new pair of jeans,

and that would be plenty.

But then Daddy hands me a small package.

I tear it open and find

a Walkman.

I squeal in delight,

open it with shaking hands.

It's blue and silver.

Soft headphones are included in the package.
Now I can listen to tapes or the radio
anytime I want.
I love it, I tell Daddy.

We visit Amma in the hospital.
We bring her a pale pink sweater
and some new books.
She is still very tired and weak
so she spends most of her time sleeping,
and we spend the time watching her sleep
and breathe
on her own.
And it is the best Christmas present.

Mix Tape

When we return from the hospital,
there's a small package left on our front porch
wrapped in red and green
with my name on it.
Sunny? I wonder.
But we already exchanged gifts at her house last weekend.

When I run up to my room,
I open the present and find
a cassette tape.
A mix tape.
With a note:
Merry Christmas.
The case is labeled:
For R from P
He's written the names of all the songs he's put on the tape.

Side A:
Rio
Girls Just Want to Have Fun
She Blinded Me With Science
Our House
Sweet Dreams (Are Made of This)

Come Dancing
The Safety Dance
Faithfully
Time After Time

Side B:
Photograph
All Night Long
Flashdance . . . What a Feeling
Every Breath You Take
One on One
Total Eclipse of the Heart
Overkill
True
Always Something There to Remind Me

It must have taken Pete hours to do this,
to tape songs off the radio,
then transfer them to another tape in the right order.
All the music we've listened to together,
the most perfect, perfect gift.
I place the tape in my new Walkman and snap it closed.
I want to listen forever.

Prema Auntie's Little Sister

Sometimes while we sit and watch Amma sleep,
Prema Auntie talks about what Amma was like as a girl:
Beautiful
Headstrong
Loud.
She argued so much with her own mother that she gave my pati
  headaches.
But when my pati fell ill,
Amma became so quiet,
they all wished she would shout again.
Amma studied English literature in college.
She was not interested in getting married young
and moving to her husband's family's house,
not like me, says Prema Auntie.
She rejected all the boys our family had her meet.
But when they arranged for her to meet your father,
and she listened to his laugh,
and heard he was going to America,
she insisted they get married right away
before he came here and changed his mind.
She quit college on purpose? Not because she was forced to? I ask.
It was her decision, Prema Auntie says.
And now, people are choosing their own partners,

and families have to listen.
India is changing.

Maybe if she hadn't come here,
she wouldn't be sick like this, I say.
That we do not know, says Prema Auntie. *What we do know is*
if she hadn't married your father,
hadn't come to America,
she wouldn't have you.
And that would have been the greatest loss of all.

What Amma Needs Next

The second round of chemo hasn't worked.
Dr. Andrews says that we will try another round,
with even stronger doses.
And if we can tamp the cancer down,
in what she calls *remission*,
Amma will have a chance.
But even if the third round of chemo works,
there is still another step we might take
to give Amma the best chance possible.
It's called a *bone marrow transplant*.

All of us have marrows filled with cells,
cells that will become red cells, white cells, platelets,
and some cells that can become any of them,
called *stem cells*.
They're like you, Dr. Andrews says to me.
You can be anything you want to be. You haven't yet decided.

Those stem cells can be taken from one person
and given to another.
But in order for them to fill their new home
with new blood cells,
the recipient's bone marrow needs to be wiped completely clean,

knocked to zero cells.

That sounds dangerous, I say.

Dr. Andrews nods. *It is. But it might be your mom's best chance.*

Who can donate marrow? I ask.

Anyone can, but their blood proteins need to match.

The best chance is from a sibling, a sister or brother.

My heart beats in my ears.

Tell me what I must do, says Prema Auntie.

The Surprise

As the snow falls in late January,
Amma starts a third cycle of chemotherapy
and Prema Auntie has her blood drawn.
I spend my days
taking tests,
working on projects,
trying to keep my head above
the river of worry I swim in every day.
Rachel keeps me on track with all my schoolwork.
Sunny shows me the latest music videos and models new outfits
    from the mall.
Pete borrows my Amar Chitra Kathas and lends me his comic
    books.

Finally,
Dr. Andrews comes to Amma's room with news.
Perhaps we should discuss this without Reha in the room, she says.
I want to stay, I insist.
Reha . . . says Daddy.
I need to hear the news, I say.
It concerns you, Prema, says Dr. Andrews.
Prema Auntie looks at me. *It is okay for Reha to stay.*
And I breathe again.

Dr. Andrews says, *I have bad news and good news.*

The bad news:

Prema Auntie isn't a match for Amma. She cannot be the bone marrow donor.

The good news:

Prema Auntie is pregnant.

Shock

Oh, Prema! Amma's face lights up.

Tears stand in her eyes. *After all this time waiting.*

This cannot be, says Prema Auntie, clutching her sari.

It definitely is, says Dr. Andrews. *You're only thirty-seven.*

It's certainly not impossible.

Prema Auntie sits. *We thought we were fated to be childless.*

Thoughts and feelings swirl inside me like a whirlpool.

My aunt's dream is finally coming true,

but my family's dream is being shattered.

I am happy for Prema Auntie and Vinod Uncle. I would love
    to have a baby cousin.

But what about Amma?

We can look for other donors, says Dr. Andrews.

But it's unlikely that anyone who is not Indian will be a match.

Daddy's forehead creases.

We know other Indian people, I say. *They can do more than just
    cook food.*

No One

We call Rupa Auntie,
who calls everyone else,
and soon everyone we know,
those we know well
those we see only twice a year
men and women,
dozens of people,
come to the hospital to get tested.
But
no one is a match.

Then I have an idea.
Test me, I say. *I'm also related to Amma.*

Dr. Andrews shakes her head.
*You are half your mother, half your father. You'll only be half
    a match at best.*
But what if Amma needs the transplant?
Aren't we desperate? I ask.
Dr. Andrews runs a hand across her face.
Well, Reha, she says. *We might be.*

But If

No, kanna, Amma says.
You're a child, says Daddy.
You won't let her do this, will you? Prema Auntie asks
    Dr. Andrews.
Dr. Andrews pushes her glasses up.
Generally, we don't accept bone marrow donations from children,
    she says slowly.
See? Amma says. *I don't want you to be hurt.*
Then Dr. Andrews says the most beautiful word in the English
    language:
But
Since I am almost fourteen
Since this could be lifesaving for Amma
Since the risk to me is very low
If
I truly want to try,
and Daddy and Amma consent,
I can be tested.
And I say:
I want to try.

Hero

Pete and I sit in his kitchen.
We've finished our English essays,
and I tell him that tomorrow I'll have blood drawn
to see if I'm a match for Amma,
to see if I can donate bone marrow for a transplant.

Will it hurt? Pete asks.
And I tell him all about
how the sight of blood makes me feel,
how even thinking of it makes me woozy and disconnected.
But I want to do this for Amma.

Pete counts off on his fingers:
A hero is brave, but not without fear.
Says what they believe is right.
Works to make the world better.
Acts out of love for others.

You check all the boxes, Reha.
I don't know if it will work. If I'm a match, I say.
At least you're trying. That's the first step to being a hero.

"Time After Time" comes on the radio.

We haven't heard it since the dance.
It's like the DJ is playing it
just for us.
Pete leans toward me,
a question in his eyes.
I lean toward him, too.
Our lips meet for just a moment.

It feels like a token
he's giving me
to help me prepare
for the battle ahead.

The Needle

When the time comes to have my blood drawn,
my heart is racing,
my breathing fast,
my skin damp with sweat.
Amma has told Dr. Andrews about my fainting,
and they make me lie down to draw my blood.
But I feel strong.

The nurse comes in,
smiling,
reassuring,
telling me to turn away and not look,
that it will be quick and easy.

But I make myself watch the needle pierce my arm,
feel its sharp sting,
watch the vials fill with dark blood
my blood
and I don't feel even one bit
faint.

Close Enough

I don't know if I'll be a perfect match for Amma,
but I hope I'm close enough.
Close enough that it's worth the risk to her,
close enough to try.
If I'm close enough,
they will take my bone marrow from my hip bones.
I'll be asleep so I won't feel the pain,
not like Amma with her biopsies.
If I'm close enough,
they will give my cells to her,
so they can grow in her bone marrow,
and become cells that nourish her,
protect her,
stop the bleeding when she is hurt.

And I am proud.
    But also scared it might be painful,
      and what if the treatment doesn't work?
And I prepare.
    I eat,
    I stay away from anyone who's sick
    because I cannot even have a cold.
And I pray

in our prayer room as I light the lamps each morning
in the car on the way to school
on the top of my pages of my notebook at school, where I
    scrawl blessings
at Rachel's house, where she teaches me words in Hebrew
at Pete's house, holding his hand
with Sunny, with MTV blaring
at home, with Daddy and Prema Auntie
with Amma
with every breath I take.
I pray I will be good enough.

No matter what happens, I will always be with you, Reha, kanna.
You have my love.
You have my breath,
You have my blood.
I squeeze her
cool
whisper-gentle
hand.
I hope that
Soon
        she'll
                have
                        mine.

And I say,

Because I am here, you must stay.

Savitri, Part 4

Lord Yama, the God of Death,
Dharmaraja, the King of Duty,
prepared once again to take away Satyavan's soul.
Please, O Lord, said Savitri,
do not take my husband away.
Impressed more than ever by her virtue, Lord Yama said:
O remarkable and faithful wife,
ask again for anything and it shall be yours.
Grant me many children, said Savitri.
It shall be so, said Lord Yama.

Then you cannot take my husband,
for he is the only one I will ever marry
and without him I cannot have children.

So be it, said Lord Yama with a smile.

Savitri looked down
Satyavan stirred in her lap
and opened his eyes.
Have I been asleep long? What a strange dream I had, he said.

Lord Yama was gone.

Savitri and Satyavan had a long and happy marriage.
They moved back to their kingdom,
and their long years were filled with delight,
as they had many children.

The Story I Want to Tell

is one where I'm a perfect match for Amma,
a miracle,
a hero.
The story I want to tell
is one where we live happily ever after.

But that is not the story I can tell.

I'm not a perfect match.
I am only
half
good enough.

We cannot do the bone marrow transplant.

Why not? I ask Dr. Andrews
as my insides boil.
Isn't a half match better than nothing?

She puts her hand on my shoulder,
talks to me like I'm a grown-up.
The oath I took, Reha,
says

First do no harm.
And she explains that
cells can heal,
and cells can hurt.
My own cells, if transplanted,
could attack Amma's body.

We tried, Reha, says Dr. Andrews. *That's all we could do.*

I don't get to be a hero,
but on a cold February day
more than three months after she first went to the hospital,
Amma is well enough
to come home.
We have finally arrived
at remission.

Watching

We bring Amma home
and we go back to normal life,
almost.
Amma is weak,
so she doesn't go back to work,
doesn't trust her painful hands
in a laboratory.

I return to school,
Daddy returns to work,
and I still spend some afternoons with Pete and Rachel.
But when I'm home, I watch.

Prema Auntie feeds Amma
until the pink comes back to her face,
her breathing eases.
Amma's hair grows back
and it is curly,
so she asks me for styling tips.
She cannot grip the spoon for long enough
to make her carrot halwa.
But Prema Auntie helps her,
and so do I,

and so does Daddy.

Every evening, we cook together,

eat together,

and afterward,

Amma picks up her sewing.

We're back to *Family Ties* on Thursday nights,

and we let Alex P. Keaton make us all laugh.

And I watch.

April comes,

and I celebrate my fourteenth birthday

with Sunny, Rachel, and Pete.

I wear a dress that Amma has made for me,

red flowers in a field of white.

It fits me perfectly.

We have enough cheese pizza to feed the whole neighborhood,

and of course, cake and ice cream.

We see a movie called *Footloose*

which is about a bunch of kids

whose parents don't want them to listen to music

and dance.

And I watch.

Prema Auntie's belly swells just a little,

and Amma and I go to the doctor with her,

listen to a heartbeat like a galloping horse,
see grainy black-and-white images of
the baby swimming inside her.

And then Prema Auntie is on a plane back to India,
where we promise to visit in the summer,
just like we planned.

Once Prema Auntie leaves,
Amma goes back to writing aerogrammes.

We are happy.
And I watch.

I'm the first to see it
when Amma begins to feel sick again.

Dr. Andrews

is at the nurses' station in the middle of the hospital floor.

Usually, she is writing in a chart,

looking at a printout,

or talking to a nurse.

But tonight,

she is just

sitting

and staring

at the counter.

I come to her, and she looks up.

There are new lines in her young face.

Is it hard? I ask. *Taking care of patients who are so sick?*

Yes, she says simply.

After a pause,

Sometimes we can save people in ways that weren't possible

just a few years ago.

But sometimes,

no matter what treatments we have,

it's not enough.

I'm sorry.

It's okay, I say.

And I mean it.

You try. That's important.

It's another part of being a hero.

The River

A mother is like life's blood
Nourishing you
Protecting you
Helping you stop hurting

Until
she
is
gone.

I am still here,
but she cannot stay.

Goodbye

In our family,
there are no funerals.
Later, we will bring Amma's ashes to India
to spread in a holy place.
Now we have a puja in our home
and everyone is invited
to remember Amma.

And all the pieces of my life,
the streams that seemed so separate,
have flowed together.
In our house are gathered
Sunny and Rupa Auntie and all our Indian friends,
Rachel and the kids from school,
Pete, Penelope, and Mrs. Brown,
Amma's colleagues from work,
Daddy's group of engineers,
and even Dr. Andrews.

We say goodbye to Amma.
I am empty.
I've been watching and saying goodbye
for months.

Jealous

I have two lives.
The one Before
and the one After.
And I am jealous of the whole world.
I see Sunny,
Rachel,
Pete,
strangers on the street,
and burn with envy
because they have mothers,
and I don't.

I don't wish anyone ill,
I want my friends to be happy.
But the unfairness of what has happened
to Amma
to my family
to me
smolders in me like a hot coal,
unquenchable.

I am angry.
Angry that Amma

won't see me start high school,
won't see me go to college.
She'll never teach me her secret
to rolling round chapatis,
sewing a straight seam,
twisting a French braid.
She'll never see me married in a red silk sari,
never hold my children
in her arms.

I'm jealous of the time when I believed
all these things
were in my future.

Total Eclipse of the Heart

I stop talking to everyone.
Pete,
Rachel,
Sunny.
I do my work at school,
but I don't raise my hand.
I don't answer when I'm called on.
I look forward to the time
when school will be over,
when I can just be at home
by myself.
The school counselor calls me to her office,
says sympathetic words.
I say nothing.
I'm so good at being quiet.

Daddy and I just exist.

Amma
gave me life,
nourished me,
protected me,
healed me.

But I couldn't do the same
for her.
My blood
wasn't good enough.

I stumble through
my eighth-grade graduation
wearing white.
I'd trade all the dresses in the mall
for just one more made by her.

I don't know what I want to be anymore.
I can't imagine growing up without her.

Amma, I think.
And that is when it hurts.

The sight of green grass,
buds bursting into bloom,
hurts
because she won't see it.
The sound of laughter on TV,
music on the radio
hurts
because she won't hear it.

Moonlight and starlight
hurt
most of all,
piercing my skin in icy shards.

I am a fleck floating
like dust
in a beam of
darkness.

What does the sky do
when the moon is gone
forever?

Comfortably Numb

I have a cough and a familiar ache in my chest
I tell Daddy I'm going to bed
lie back on the pillow
and welcome the overwhelming exhaustion.
My eyes shut like heavy doors
I can't crack open.
I fall into a sleep so deep
the wind whispers through the grass,
a lazy river winds its way in twilight.
I dream for days, for miles,
across space,
across time,
through infrared and ultraviolet
through constellations
a kaleidoscopic dream
Until
a dark hand appears,
a hand full of promises.

And I hear my name.

Amma?

I reach for the hand,

and

I wake to soaking clothes

Daddy's eyes full of concern

his large hand holding mine.

He picks me up and takes me to the doctor.

And later, when I've taken antibiotics

and fever-reducing medication,

Daddy lays me in my bed again,

and the sheets smell like fresh laundry

and there are many cozy pillows

and a tray with juice and cookies

and Daddy takes my hand once again.

I promise I will be both father and mother to you.

I will take care of you, kanna.

Always.

I fall asleep holding his hand

and reach for no others in my dream.

The Phone Call

On a beautiful June morning,
we get a phone call from India.
Prema Auntie has had a healthy baby girl.
And they will name her Chandra,
which means *moon*.

Savitri, Part 5

No one ever talks about
the very end of Savitri's story.
But I imagine
after many long years,
many accomplishments,
many children and grandchildren,
one day,
Savitri and Satyavan
once again met
Lord Yama, the God of Death,
Dharmaraja, the King of Duty,
and took his dark hand willingly.
Because that is the end
of every person's story.

Aerogramme

It comes in the mail, addressed to me
a month to the date after she left us.
A blue aerogramme, just like the ones Amma used to send
to Prema Auntie.
I recognize her handwriting,
and I wonder how she sent it from wherever she is.
It's stamped from just yesterday.
I don't bother going inside. I pry it open
carefully
standing next to the mailbox
in the moist June air.

Dear Reha,

*I asked Dr. Andrews to send this letter so you receive it a month
after I've left this world and gone on to the next one. I lost my own
mother when I was young, though not as young as you, and I don't
imagine that a month will completely heal this wound. But I hope
you're in a better position to understand what I have to say.*

*I didn't want to leave you. And it's not anyone's fault. Not the
doctors', not your father's, not mine. And certainly not yours. Your
insistence on giving me your bone marrow was one of the bravest
things I've ever seen anyone do. It showed me what a strong and
steadfast young woman you've already grown into, kanna.*

You are everything I ever hoped for in a child. You are brilliant, and you are courageous, and you are finding your voice in the world. God willing, you will go on to live a long, happy, and incredible life.

I know that even before I fell sick, you've been struggling with some things. You may not think I understood, but I did. You have been wondering how to navigate the challenges of belonging to two worlds: India and America, the place where your father and I grew up, and the place where you are growing up. This struggle is real, and it is normal. In many ways, I lived through the same struggles when I was younger—loving my parents so much, but wanting something different from what they had. Perhaps we all face the same types of struggles as we grow from children into adults.

I chose to come to this country. In fact, when I learned your father was moving to America, I quit college and married him as soon as I could. I wanted to come to a place where there were more possibilities for me. And I wanted to raise my children in a place where, boy or girl, the whole world was open to them.

It hasn't always been easy living so far from those I love. It hasn't always been easy being different. I'm sorry I was hard on you for wanting the normal things a girl your age wants: to be like her friends. I'm sorry for clinging to some ideas that have changed even in India. I did it because I was afraid that you would forget where we are from, our values, our way of life.

But I know you never will.

You, my girl, should take your gifts and your hard work and do whatever you want with them. Be a doctor, if you like. Or be a poet, or an actress, or a mother who stays at home with her children. Or all of these things together. Surround yourself with good people, and be happy.

And know this: you belong. You belong to this country, where you are growing up. And you belong to India, where your blood is from. You belong to both, and they both belong to you. You will find your way in making those two streams one. You will write your own story, and it will be beautiful, because it is yours.

I'm sorry I can't help you with the difficult times. I'm sorry I won't be there to celebrate all your successes.

But know that I love you, my star, my dear one, my darling. Know that you are already everything I hoped you would be, and more.

And know that I am your blood. Wherever you go, I will be with you.

Take care of yourself, my beautiful daughter. Take care of your father, as I know he will take care of you. Work hard. Be good to yourself, and reach for joy, in whatever form that takes. I am already prouder of you than you could imagine.

I love you.
Your Amma

And a small piece of Amma has flown across time and landed in my hands.

Family Ties

I take the letter inside
and find Daddy.
I read the letter out loud to him,
and it is like Amma is in the room again.

I've been watching Amma all my life.
It turns out she was watching me, too.
And she always understood.
She believed I didn't need to be split in two,
that I could be whole.
And now, I start
to believe it, too.

Daddy and I laugh and cry and talk and talk and talk
until there are no more words to say.
We eat,
and since it's Thursday,
we put on *Family Ties*.

Start

The next day I call Sunny.

Can you come over? I ask.

Then I make two more phone calls.

And soon, my three best friends are with me again.

And we tune the radio to WPOP.

Always Something There to Remind Me

Daddy and I stand behind our house.
The moon is full and bright,
the stars a dazzling river in the sky.
Next week, we leave to bring Amma
to her final resting place
in the country where she was born.
But I will always remember her here,
in the home she chose.
I raise my hands to the studded sky,
to the future Amma wanted for me,
                              and I embrace the field of light.
We go inside and sit down to dinner.
And I see God in Daddy's smile,
hear God in the echo of his voice,
smell God in the scent of our good food,
feel God in the touch of his hand,
taste God in the burst of a mustard seed.

I have one life,
a stream with many tributaries.
The life given to me by my parents,
a life filled with
school and learning,

family,
and friends.

I have one life,
where I try to merge all the places I'm from,
India and America,
mother and father,
past, present,
and future.

I have one life.
That's all any of us gets.
And I know that I will make my way.
For all rivers lead to the same ocean,
we all look upon the same sky.
I will write my own story.
Amma's life, the one she gave to me,
is in my heart, my veins,
my blood.

And she is
everywhere.

AUTHOR'S NOTE

Although Reha's story is fictional, much of this novel is based on my own experiences—the sense of living in two worlds; the balance between celebrating uniqueness and wanting to be like everyone else; and bearing the worst thing you can imagine and somehow making your way through it.

The truth is, I've always felt split in two.

Growing up as an immigrant in Louisville, Kentucky, in the 1980s, I felt like a normal American girl . . . but I wasn't quite a typical American. In my home we ate different food, we sometimes wore different clothes, and we spent our weekends with our Indian community, our second family since our relatives lived half a world away. I spent my adolescence wondering which one was the "real" me: the weekday American or the weekend Indian.

I knew from a young age that I wanted to be a doctor, and that desire only grew as I went through school. Then, when I was a teen, my mother was seriously injured in a car accident. She spent months in the hospital, and my father and I spent them with her. And I realized that the world of medicine that I was so eager to enter could be a very scary place, and I wasn't sure if I still wanted to be a part of it.

When I was a kid, I read American novels, nonfiction, and comic books along with Amar Chitra Kathas—Indian comics that depicted stories from history and mythology. I loved all these books and empathized with characters from all kinds of backgrounds. But I never truly saw myself in a novel until much later, when I was an adult and read Jhumpa Lahiri's *The Namesake*, her gorgeous, multigenerational story of immigration and assimilation. That book spoke to me in a way I'd never felt before, because it wasn't about being Indian or being American but about being both. And that is the kind of book that I wanted *Red, White, and Whole* to be for young readers.

As I've gotten older, I've felt even more contradictions—as a premed government major in college, a working mother, and a doctor who writes books for children. It hasn't always been easy, but I've learned to accept this feeling of living in different worlds, because it's part of what makes me who I am, and even more important, it's what all of us feel. At some point, every single one of us wonders whether we really belong, whether we're truly good enough, and whether we're allowed to dream big.

We all contain multitudes, and not only is that okay, it is essential.

I hope you enjoyed reading this book of my heart. I hope it helps you understand that even when you feel torn apart, you can still be a whole person—not just despite the things you struggle with, but because of them.

ACKNOWLEDGMENTS

This novel appeared in my head as a metaphor, and I knew I wanted to write it in verse. But I didn't know if I could.

Brent Taylor, my brilliant agent, encouraged me to write this story of my heart in the way that felt right to me. He made it clear from when I first mentioned it that he could not wait to read it. And sure enough, he dug in the very minute I sent it, live texted me throughout, and finished it a few hours later. His love for this novel made me feel like I'd already achieved what I wanted, regardless of what happened next. He is my first and best reader and helped find the absolute perfect editor and publisher for this book. Brent, I can never thank you enough for your belief in this book and in me.

Alexandra Cooper and Rosemary Brosnan blew me away with their love for this story. Alexandra's incredible editorial eye, undaunted in the midst of a pandemic, helped make this novel shine. Many thanks to the whole team at Quill Tree Books—including Allison Weintraub, editorial assistant; Kathryn Silsand, senior production editor; and Veronica Ambrose, copy editor. Erin Fitzsimmons, book designer extraordinaire, and artist Vrinda Zaveri created a cover that fits this book perfectly and is beautiful beyond my wildest dreams.

My amazing friend and critique partner Theresa Milstein listened to me talk about this story when it was still just an idea, encouraged me when I was scared, and helped me wrestle these words until they turned into something worth reading. Many thanks to my other critique partners: Alison Goldberg, Sharon Abra Hanen, Victoria Coe, Lisa Rogers, Donna Woelke, and Jaya Mehta.

My wonderful friends and poetic experts Joy McCullough and Chris Baron gave me crucial insights into making this story better. And to all my MG Novel 19s, especially my dear JPST: Gillian McDunn, Josh Levy, Nicole Panteleakos, Jessica Kramer, Cory Leonardo, and Naomi Milliner: I'm honored to be your friend.

Andrea Contos and Emily Thiede, dear friends from my Pitch Wars 2017 class, have always been incredible supports. It's been a joy to celebrate all our good news together.

Philip Amrein, MD, hematologist/oncologist at Massachusetts General Hospital, answered my questions about AML treatment in the 1980s with extreme thoroughness and patience. Any mistakes I've made in the medical aspects of this book are my own.

To my friends and teachers at Louisville Collegiate School: I treasure our time together in the 1980s. You helped shape who I am today.

Huge thanks to all my friends in the Indian community in Louisville, Kentucky, who were my second family when we were all separated from our loved ones who lived so far away.

To my extended family in India and now across the world: more than any place I could name, you have been my home. I hope I make you proud.

My husband, Lou, and children, Joe and Mira, have been so supportive of this second career of mine, even when it meant my spending hours alone writing or days away promoting my books. You are the joy of my heart that permeates everything I do, and I couldn't write a thing without you.

This story is a love letter to my parents, Kasturi and Chakra-varthy Narasimhan, who raised me with unconditional love and the sense that the world is limitless. Unfailingly kind and joyful, they have always faced the challenges life has thrown at them with a wonderful sense of humor. Mom and Dad, you are my heroes.